Guardian
of the Dove

Cynthia J. Sebring

ISBN 978-1-64349-473-9 (paperback)
ISBN 978-1-64349-474-6 (digital)

Christian Faith Publishing, Inc.
832 Park Avenue
Meadville, PA 16335
www.christianfaithpublishing.com

Printed in the United States of America

Dedication

This book is dedicated to the loving memory of Charles and Chris Watt who welcomed me as a guest in their home in the fishing village of Portessie during my first trip to Scotland so many years ago. For their kindness and hospitality, I am forever grateful, especially since that travel experience served as a source of inspiration for this story.

But ask the animals, and they will teach you, or the birds in the sky and they will tell you or speak to the earth, and it will teach you, or let the fish in the sea inform you. Which of all these does not know that the hand of the Lord has done this? In his hand is the life of every creature and the breath of all mankind. (Job 12:7–10)

Chapter 1

How energizing, how overwhelmingly satisfying to feel truly alive for the first time. Stephen adjusted his knapsack filled with his camping gear with a rolled-up tent, sleeping bag, and blankets tied to the back. He took a hiatus from his long walk and gazed out over the seemingly endless vastness of green landscape of the Scottish Highlands.

"Some of my philosophy professors were wrong," Stephen thought. "None of this is an accident. This is all the result of God's organized, creative handiwork." He felt a part of the natural setting, a connection to the life all around him and yet realized that man was so much more, a being capable of a relationship with the Creator himself.

Stephen thought to himself that like the layout of a perfectly planned painting with its elements placed strategically for maximum effect, the beauty of life lies not only in the proper placement of events, the inclusion of loving deeds, the rise of unexpected surprises, and the embrace of eternal truths, but in all the empty spaces in between that offer perspective. This wide-open terrain, these empty spaces void of entanglements, offered him exactly what he needed: perspective. Spring had bid a fond farewell to its final stages, and the warmer days of summer had begun to creep their way in silently forward.

Taking in a deep breath of invigorating morning air, Stephen closed his eyes and thanked God for the opportunity of leaving the corporate world behind to try and discover a different calling on his life, away from the constant din of the city, endless miles of traffic, car exhaust that choked the air, and skyscrapers that blocked the sun. Metropolitan trappings were all aimed at fortune finding, a secular maze strangling its unsuspecting victims, while offering an illusion of everlasting power and prestige.

Merely surviving as a pawn in a game without end, a nine-to-five existence, coupled with a rigid schedule as a new bank associate, was exhausting and agitating with executive demands that disturbed even his private thoughts and dreams. Somewhere in his attempt to please everyone but himself, he had lost his own sense of identity, his own purpose. At this point in life, an exodus into the wilderness to reflect and somehow regain a sense of direction seemed the only option.

Here, there was stillness. Only the occasional barn swallow or bullfinch would sing out. A flock of Canadian geese would soar overhead. The colorful wildflowers bloomed in the meadows. Now and then, a rabbit was seen sunning itself. In higher elevations, he had photographed mountain goats and enjoyed majestic vistas in all directions. Tranquility abounded. Simplifying life had helped him simplify his thoughts. Here, he had no interruptions, no distractions. No phone calls. No outrageous expectations. In the wild, he could choose where to place his full attention.

He realized it was going to take longer than expected to reach the next youth hostel, but that was of no consequence. That just meant more time to surround himself with nature, more chances to learn how to relax, to envelop his mind with beauty. Besides, in the summer, even in Scotland, wrapped in the warmth of his sleeping bag, Stephen did not mind falling asleep under the stars: the mariner's map, the poet's muse, God's artistry.

Stephen brushed his brown, shoulder-length hair to one side. He had not cut it in almost a year, since he left his job. Somehow it felt liberating and natural to just let it grow.

Taking an apple out of his backpack, he bit into it, relishing the cool, crisp taste. Down over an embankment, he could hear a stream flowing and decided to use the opportunity to replenish his water supply and get a cool drink. By the creek, he knelt down, filled his canteen, a plastic jug, and then a metal drinking cup. The cool water felt wonderful going down, cleansing the dryness from his throat. As he stood up, he watched a small herd of red deer walk across a field about sixty yards away. Although they were fairly common in the Highlands, Stephen had not noticed them before, so he delighted in observing their serene strides along the terrain as they grazed intermittently.

Reflecting on the beauty of the day, Stephen headed down a path in hopes of taking more photos of animals and flora for his collection. It was sunny, in the low sixties, ideal weather for Scotland. Actually, he was accustomed to these long walks in all kinds of weather. In previous years, in various seasons, he had hiked parts of the Appalachian Trail, gone backpacking in the Swiss Alps, traversed through major expanses of Denali National Park, ventured into the Yukon, and trekked across the provinces of Alberta and

British Columbia, sometimes alone and other times with friends.

On previous trips to Scotland, Stephen had photographed the boyhood home of Ian Fleming, the author of the James Bond stories. He had also visited Dunbar, the birthplace of John Muir, the naturalist. Stephen marveled at the thought of how John Muir was an inspiration to Teddy Roosevelt to establish national parks in America. Afterward, he had hiked the John Muir Way.

In addition, one summer, north of San Francisco, Stephen had hiked through the famous Muir Woods, a densely forested area filled with California redwoods. In some areas, the trees were so close together it looked like night. In fact, he actually saw an owl hunting in the middle of the day.

On another trip to Scotland, Stephen had hiked to a valley near Ben Nevis, the highest mountain in the UK. Last summer he had backpacked around the area of Loch Ness and Inverness. Afterward, he had visited some of the small seaport towns north of there. So for Stephen, one or two more months of hiking were becoming part of a normal way of life.

Somehow this trip made Stephen feel like he had entered a new world, an oasis of peace, the same way Adam must have felt, walking alone through paradise with only God and the animals for company.

While pausing to snap a few photos of the landscape and wildlife, Stephen reflected on the words to a song he heard many times growing up and sang softly to himself. "When through the woods and forest glades I wander and hear the birds sing sweetly in the trees, when I look down from lofty mountain grandeur and hear the brook and feel the gentle breeze." Stephen smiled and said, "Yes, Lord. How great thou art." Using his walking poles, Stephen continued across open terrain. This area was almost completely flat, allowing him to keep up a steady pace.

By late afternoon, a short distance from a country road and about fifteen yards off the hiking trail, Stephen had found an ideal spot for a campground and began the process of setting up his tent. As a precautionary measure, he faced the tent in the opposite direction of any wind gusts that might come off the mountains at night. After erecting his shelter, Stephen securely anchored the tent stakes into the ground.

Next, he began making preparations for a modest meal. After constructing a circle with stones, he proceeded to build a small campfire and cook some fish he had caught that morning. He planned to go fishing the next day too, since this was another one of his favorite outdoor sports. Stephen cleaned and filleted the fish, breaded the two pieces lightly, and put them into a small cast iron frying pan with some oil. He cooked the fillets evenly on both sides, adding a little salt and pepper. Along with the fish, he enjoyed some dried apricots, and a cup of water. It was a simple dinner but satisfying.

After he finished eating, he poured water over the campfire and covered it with dirt. Next, he rolled out his sleeping bag on the ground and stretched out on top of it in the sunshine for a late afternoon nap. Looking up at a beautiful expanse of sky and clouds, Stephen remembered a saying by John Muir: In every walk with nature one receives far more than he seeks.

"That has certainly been the case for me," Stephen thought. Closing his eyes, he visualized the horizons and wildlife he had encountered that day. As he lay there, drifting off, fatigue melted away like the snow during a spring thaw, gradually and steadily, eventually leaving no trace that it had ever been there. Unfortunately, he had become so captivated by the beauty and serenity of the day that he failed to notice two men who had been watching him from a short distance away.

Chapter 2

Although most tourists, like Stephen, associated Scotland primarily with first class golf, beautiful vistas, and ancient traditions, it actually has always been a place filled with incredible hospitality. A number of mission houses, some with historical roots dating back centuries, remained open to assist those in need.

Pastor Rich Hunter, his wife Joyce, and their two sons, Mark and Eric, resided at a Christian mission in the Highlands. Tucked away in a forested area, it was not visible at all from the road, but the locals knew of the compassionate work Pastor Rich and Pastor James McGregor, the head rector, had done for the youth and the needy of the surrounding areas. James, an American with Scottish ancestry, in his mid-thirties, had worked with Rich and his wife for the past ten years and had helped them establish the mission. The son of a minister, James had felt called to return to the birthplace of his parents to evangelize in the same region as his father had in previous years.

The mission house, a large brick structure, complete with a church attached at one end, offered its resources as a retreat center and a bed and breakfast with weekly Bible studies and Sunday worship. A number of rooms for guest accommodations were available, all free for the asking, thanks to the generous financial support of several

Presbyterian churches. Hikers were common guests to the mission which advertised its services in brochures. Many guests also chose to stay there based on recommendations from friends.

The sign over the front door read "Seek Ye First the Kingdom of God." The mission was sometimes booked for religious conferences for small groups of thirty to fifty participants from churches in the major cities like Glasgow or Edinburgh or for individuals searching for a place of renewal and a chance to grow closer to God. For those living in this remote area, the mission also served as a home church for a number of families.

In addition to spiritual outreach, hospitality ranked high on the list of priorities. Hot lunches, which always included some combination of sandwiches, soup, and homemade bread, were available daily for anyone who was hungry. The mission was staffed with volunteers, usually local residents. Pastor Rich's wife, Joyce, also liberally donated her time.

On this particular afternoon, Pastor Rich and his two boys, ages seven and five, were coming back to the mission after an outing to get homemade ice cream in the nearby village. Both boys had done excellent work in their respective classes at school, so their father decided a small reward was in order.

Taking advantage of the superb weather, they had decided to walk the mile to the village and back instead of taking the family car. The paths extended for miles and were often used by hikers as well as locals. The two boys had hiked these paths with their father many times, singing songs, looking for bugs under rocks, making up stories, conversing with their dad about their friends, informing him about school activities, and playing all sorts of games along the way.

Last week, the two of them pretended they were in a race with Eric Liddell, the Scottish Olympic gold medalist in the 400-meter race and missionary to China. Each of them took turns establishing new finish lines in the distance which they raced toward with all their might. Afterward, they argued over which one of them would grow up to be as fast as Eric Liddell. Eventually, they decided that just being able to run fast would be enough. Of course, neither of the boys had eliminated the possibility of running the race of evangelism and becoming a missionary like their dad had already encouraged them to do.

This day, as they returned home, the two of them pretended to be explorers, blazing trails through an unknown land. In their wild imaginations, the forests became a dense jungle, the fields an undiscovered country. As they walked along, they debated over which one should be named Dr. Livingston, a Scottish missionary and medical pioneer whom Mark had heard about in school.

"You got to play him last time," said Mark.

"No, you did. I just got to be your assistant," replied Eric.

"No, you weren't. I was," Mark insisted.

"Boys, it's just a game. It doesn't matter," said Pastor Rich gently.

As they walked along, Eric pointed to a field to their left. "Remember when we had a picnic there last summer? Remember the roast beef Mom fixed? Remember her bread? I love her bread. That was a good day. I liked that.

Can we do it again? Can we?" asked Eric, half walking and half skipping, overflowing with enthusiasm.

"Of course, we can. We could have a special outing for your mother's birthday next month. I know she would love to spend the day outside, if the weather's good. How does that sound?" Pastor Rich asked.

"Great," said Eric. "I love birthday parties. I love cake, especially chocolate." Spying some wildflowers on the path, he ran on ahead to pick them.

His father called out, "Don't go too far, Eric. Stay where I can see you."

"The picnic will be great if you do the cooking and give Mom the whole day to relax," said Mark.

Pastor Rich considered his son's comment and reflected on his wife's diligent efforts at the mission. Joyce never complained about anything. Unexpected guests, extra cooking, additional cleaning, his unanticipated departures to preach in other counties. At times the mission was packed with guests that had extensive visits. Bedding had to be cleaned, towels had to be washed and folded, meals had to be prepared on a large scale, and sometimes the unexpected happened like the day a group of ten hikers showed up unannounced hoping for a place to spend the night. Fortunately, the mission was able to accommodate them, but of course, it also meant additional work. No matter what, Joyce never raised an objection. She was truly dedicated to the mission's cause of outreach to strangers.

"That's a good idea, Mark. I will definitely do all the cooking and preparations for the picnic. It will make her feel special."

Father and son walked slowly along the path in the sunshine. "So, Mark, how is soccer practice? Are you getting along with your coach?"

"Oh, yes, Dad. Coach MacLeod is wonderful. He's teaching me how to kick harder and aim better. I scored two goals last week. I just wish I could run faster."

"Two goals? That's wonderful. Don't worry about speed. It will come with time and practice. You're taller than last year. That makes a difference too," said his father.

Mark paused a moment. He had not thought about that aspect of this success. "That's true. We start passing drills next week. I'm looking forward to that. Charles wants to be my partner for the drills," said Mark.

"Charles? That's one of your friends?" asked his father inquisitively.

"Yeah, Charles is great. He just started last week, but he's fast. He's really nice too. Can he come by and visit the mission sometime?"

His father smiled. "Absolutely. Your mother and I would enjoy meeting him. You can invite him for dinner if you want. Just be sure to let your mother know in advance so she can plan."

The Hunters always encouraged their children to bring their friends to the mission. Rich and his wife taught the boys social skills in hospitality by having them serve meals and refreshments to their friends, instead of simply sitting at the table acting like guests themselves, being waited on. The last thing either parent wanted was to raise spoiled children. After all, if they learned lessons of love and service as kids, they would be more likely to continue the practice as adults.

By this time, they had caught up to Eric who had gathered a dozen blue wildflowers. He held up his fresh bouquet triumphantly. "These are Mom's favorite," he shouted with delight.

"Yes, they are. And she will love them," his father replied fervently. Pastor Rich gazed up at the gorgeous afternoon sky, blue and almost cloudless. He paused and then tipped his head back for a moment to feel the warmth of the sun directly on his face. Living this far north, locals regarded a day full of sunshine as a beautiful and rare commodity, never to be taken for granted.

Mark had continued walking on ahead, always looking for the next adventure. Moving back into an Eric Liddell mode again, Mark had selected a new finish line up ahead. "Hey, Eric," called Mark. "Race you to the other side of that rock," pointing to a boulder about forty yards away.

Without responding, Eric took off at top speed, flowers held tightly in his hand. His older brother always won these impromptu contests, so he thought maybe today with a head start he would have a chance of beating him. Full of determination, feet flying, Eric managed to sprint beyond the rock a split second ahead of Mark. Turning around to face his brother, jumping up and down, arms stretched straight up in the air, Eric shouted ecstatically, "I win! I win! Victory!" Mark made no reply but instead stood staring off toward a clearing behind his brother, his eyes wide in disbelief. "Dad, come here quick!"

The urgency in Mark's voice compelled his father to race in his direction. When he reached the other side of the rock, to his horror, Rich stood facing the body of an unconscious man lying face up out in the open. His shirt was half torn off. His hair was disheveled. His body and face were covered with dirt, cuts, and bruises. He lay motionless. Rich squatted down beside the body, held the man's wrist checking for a pulse, and sighed with relief.

He looked up at his two sons, who stood there petrified, not knowing what to think, wondering what to do next. "Mark, run home and get James. Tell your mother to call the doctor." Without hesitation, Mark took off for the mission; from there, it was a mere fifty-yard dash down a wooded path.

Pastor Rich looked into the man's face and held his hand. "Sir, can you hear me?" There was no response. Looking at the man, still holding the flowers in one hand, Eric stood teary-eyed and hugged his father about the neck. "Dad, is he … is he dead?" Rich embraced his son around the waist and looked into his sad eyes. "No, dear. He's not."

The man groaned and took in a deep breath and let it out slowly. Eric, holding his dad a little snugger around the neck, asked, "Dad, is this a good time to pray?" Although Eric was only five, he displayed a tremendous amount of empathy for others, a trait he had witnessed in his parents numerous times. Pastor Rich looked adoringly at his young son, brushed his reddish-brown bangs away from his eyes, and kissed his cheek. "Yes, sweetheart," he whispered. "Pray very hard. Ask Jesus to help him."

Noticing the remains of a campfire, Rich stood up, walked over to the fire ring, and knelt down, placing his hands a few inches over the stones. He could feel heat radiating off them. He stood up, inspecting the area, looking for any personal belongings the man might have had with him. To his disappointment, the area was totally void of camping equipment, food, clothes, and supplies.

Scanning the area in all directions as far as the horizon, he watched for movement and listened carefully. He saw no one. There was not a sound. Aside from a dozen deer in the adjacent field and a few soaring birds, there was no sign of life. Whoever did this was long gone. Rich returned to Eric who hugged his dad around the knees. The man on the ground mumbled a few incoherent words and made a feeble attempt to move his legs and arms and then laid still.

James appeared within minutes, astonished at the dreadful sight. "God help us. Please tell me he isn't dead," looking at Rich for confirmation.

"He's alive. He's been moving and even tried to speak once. He's just too weak. The stones around that campfire over there are still hot, so he hasn't been here for too long."

James sized up the situation. "Let's get him inside. I'll carry him. You go on ahead. Find a room that's available." Pastor Rich scooped up Eric in his arms and took off for the mission.

Despite the man's condition, he became aware that two powerful arms had delicately picked him up. Somehow, intuitively, he felt safe. Upon arriving at the mission, Pastor Rich met James at the door and pointed to the available guestroom. Taking precautions not to cause any needless pain or additional injury, James laid the young man down gently on the bed and looked at Rich.

"Do you have any idea who he is?" asked James feeling perplexed.

Rich shook his head. "No, I've never seen him before. He's not from around here that's for certain." The combined population of the neighboring villages totaled only about 250 residents, making it fairly easy for the locals to recognize an outsider.

James looked back at the young man and then turned to Rich. "I have to attend to another guest this evening, but I'll be back shortly."

A moment later, Joyce appeared and stood in the doorway, staring at the man on the bed. "I called the doctor. He will get here as soon as he can. I told him basically what happened based on what Mark told me." Joyce sighed. "That poor man, how awful."

Pastor Rich kissed his wife on the forehead. "Thank you for phoning, dear. How are the boys taking this?"

"They were a bit shook up. I asked them to help out in the kitchen. I thought giving them something to do would help take their minds off the matter. I think they will be fine. They're always resilient."

Rich regarded the man's pitiful state. "I'm glad the doctor was available to come. In the meantime, let's get him cleaned up."

As Pastor Rich took off his jacket and rolled up his shirt sleeves, Joyce returned a moment later with a bowl of water, a clean towel, soap, and a washcloth. The pastor ever so carefully removed the remains of the man's tattered shirt. Underneath were more cuts and bruises.

As her husband began the delicate process, Joyce brought a chair in from another room and placed it at the foot of the bed. A loyal and dedicated partner in this ministry, Joyce prayed silently for the man's recovery as well as for the restoration of her own composure. She still felt distraught that anyone would have to endure such a terrible beating. Living a life sheltered from the barbarisms of the outside world, inhumane treatment came as a total shock to an otherwise tranquil existence.

Rich dipped the washcloth in the warm water, rubbed on some soap, and gently pressed the cloth on the young man's cuts, gradually removing blood and dirt. It was a slow, repetitive process, but necessary to avoid inflicting further injury while at the same time preventing infection. Rich then rinsed the washcloth and repeated the process all over the man's face, neck, and chest. Next, he used only water to clean the wounds thoroughly, removing all the soap. After that, he lightly pressed down with the towel to dry the man off. Finally, he handed the soiled items to Joyce. During the entire procedure, the young man never once moved. "That's about all we can do for right now," he told his wife.

A half hour later, Dr. John Campbell, who lived about forty minutes away, arrived to examine the young man. Rich, who had been sitting beside the man since James brought him inside, informed the doctor that the man's breathing was more regular now. After registering the other guest, James returned to the room and stood watching while the doctor examined the patient.

After looking him over, Dr. Campbell told the pastors, "He has no serious injuries aside from that black eye. No sign of broken bones. No bruising or swelling on his head. Normal heart rate. No fever." Joyce smiled up at her husband and sighed with relief.

Dr. Campbell glanced back at the young man. "Whoever cleaned him up did a good job of washing his cuts. Fortunately, none of them are deep enough to require stiches. For right now, I think we should just let him rest.

Keep that cold compress on his eye. I recommend someone stay here and watch him just in case there are any changes. When he first wakes up, don't let him stand right away, at least not on his own. He might feel dizzy. You can give him some pain killers if he needs them."

The doctor got up to leave and handed James a bottle. "With the nearest hospital several hours away, this is the best place for him. Basically, he's a young, strong man. With rest, he should be fine, but to stay on the safe side, it's better not to move him. Call me again, if you need to."

As he headed for the door, Dr. Campbell looked back at the patient and then turned to Rich. "He's lucky you found him."

The pastor smiled and said with assurance, "It was providence, sir. Luck had nothing to do with it."

Pastor James thanked the doctor for coming and looked painfully into Rich's eyes. "I have to leave to preach tomorrow at another parish for an outreach program, but I will be here in the evening. I'm sorry I have to be gone at a time like this."

Pastor Rich nodded. "You do what you have to. Get your sermon ready. I'll stay with him tonight. I'll fix up a chair with some pillows and monitor his condition. Besides, when he wakes up, he will have no idea where he is. He'll want to talk with somebody." James thanked him and headed down the hall.

For Joyce, looking at the man's unfortunate state was heartbreaking. "Why would anyone do this?" Rich had moved a chair from the corner of the room next to the bed.

"He had no identification on him, no wallet, no money, no gear, no supplies, nothing. Looks to me like a robbery."

Joyce sighed and told her husband, "I'll start dinner. I'll bring you a plate when it's ready." Rich smiled and sat down on the chair across from the young man. He opened up his Bible to read as part of his evening devotions.

A half hour later, Joyce returned with a tray and a plate of baked salmon, potatoes, and turnips and set it on the nightstand. Her husband thanked her, said grace, and proceeded to delight in another of his wife's delicious specialties. As he ate, he kept watching for any signs that the young man might wake up. "Please, God. Let him recover. Let it be soon," he prayed quietly.

After dinner, Rich opened his prayer book and began lifting up silent supplications to the Almighty. He had used this same prayer book during another all-night vigil when Mark had come down with a serious virus and a dangerously high fever. The doctor thought he would not live through the night, but Mark recuperated and his parents attributed his total restoration to the Lord's mercy. Once again, a steady stream of prayers made its way up to heaven.

In between prayers, he continued to check on the young man's condition and to see if had awakened. He remained fast asleep, breathing deeply. After hours of prayer for healing, Rich offered up one last petition. "Lord, if this young man does not know you, help him seek you. I know you have already been seeking him. If he does know you, Lord, let him grow in grace, peace, and virtue. Bless his future. Amen."

Chapter 3

The next morning, the new arrival awoke to find himself in a warm room with a cool cloth across one side of his face. Slowly removing the cloth, he reached up and touched the area around his eye. It felt sore and swollen. Next to him, he saw a man wearing a clerical collar asleep in a chair covered in a blanket.

Lying on his back, the young patient turned his head to see a large nightstand next to the bed with a lamp, a Bible, a glass of water, and a small arrangement of blue flowers like the ones he had seen in the fields. The clock on the nightstand indicated it was almost 10:00 a.m. At the opposite side of the room, sunlight was shining in through a window. To one side of the window was a small dresser. Glancing down, he noticed he had been covered with wool blankets. They were thick and heavy and bore the design of some Scottish tartan. His hiking boots had been removed and placed on the floor across from the bed.

With some difficulty, he tried to move, but then decided against it. At that moment, Pastor Rich stirred, woke up, and saw the young man looking at him. Delighted to see an improvement in the young man's condition, the pastor said, "Good morning. Glad you're awake." Rich stretched and leaned forward in the chair looking into the man's green eyes. "You're at a Christian mission. I'm Pastor Rich Hunter. How do you feel?" The pastor's Scottish accent rang out clearly and distinctly, as easily recognizable as church bells.

Still feeling somewhat disoriented and trying to wake up, the young man tried to gather his thoughts and attempted to process the new information along with the question. Gradually, he managed to say, "My shoulder hurts and I've got a headache."

Pastor Rich stood up, folded the blanket he used for his makeshift bed, and placed it on top of the dresser. "You stay right there, and I will get you something." He walked out the door and down the hallway.

The young visitor continued to acquaint himself with his unfamiliar surroundings. On the wall opposite the bed, a plain wooden cross hung next to a picture of Jesus healing a blind man. Beneath the picture stood a wooden bookcase filled with various editions of the Bible, a concordance, books on Christ's ministry, biblical commentaries with colorful bindings, several books on missionary service, a couple prayer books, as well as an interpretation of the book of Psalms. Stephen reassured himself that if for some reason he needed to remain in bed to recover, he certainly would have plenty of reading material to pass the time. At the opposite end of the room, blue and white drapes were open revealing a double hung window. Outside, he could make out part of what he guessed was a garden with various flowers blooming.

A minute later, Pastor Rich returned with some medicine. "A doctor prescribed this for you yesterday. Let's try this and see how you do." Rich helped the young man sit up, propping his back with the pillow. The patient gladly cooperated, swallowing the pill with some water.

"Thanks. It feels like the room is spinning a bit."

"That's to be expected. Just sit still for now," responded Rich.

James stood in the doorway and smiled. "You're awake. Good." Looking somewhat surprised, Pastor Rich said, "James, you're here."

"Yes," he said. "There was a change in the schedule again. The other minister did not have to leave town after all, so now I am here for the day."

"Wonderful," said Rich. "He just took some medicine. That should help his headache."

James walked into the room. "I'm Pastor James McGregor. I work here at the mission with Rich. You're welcome to stay as long as you need. What's your name?"

The patient looked at the two pastors, amazed and relieved that two total strangers were taking such an incredible interest in his well-being. He suddenly realized if he had not been rescued, he could have died out there, exposed to the elements without food or water. At night the temperature could drop into the forties (about eight Celsius), too cold for someone with neither warm clothes nor means of shelter. The young man smiled at the pastors. "My name is Stephen LeBlanc."

James reflected on the name a moment and tried to definitively determine his accent and origin. In the summertime, for the past ten years, visitors to the mission had arrived from all over the world. "Are you French?"

"Actually, I'm French Canadian," replied Stephen. "I was raised just outside the city of Quebec."

"Good to meet you, Stephen," responded Pastor Rich.

James smiled at Stephen. "Let's get you a clean shirt. Yours was badly ripped and stained, so we had to throw it out."

At this point, Stephen was conscious enough to realize that he was sitting there on the edge of the bed wearing only a pair of jeans. "You have clothes here?" inquired Stephen in surprise, pondering the pastor's offer.

"Yes," said James. "We have clothes donated to the mission occasionally for those in need. Right now, we have quite a few items. I'm sure we have something that will fit you. I'll go check and see what we have."

Stephen gave him a grateful look. "Thanks. I really appreciate that." Stephen turned to Rich. "Were you sitting here with me all night?"

"Yes, just in case you needed something. I also said some prayers for you."

Stephen was so awed by the man's compassion that for a moment he was speechless.

James returned a couple minutes later with a white long-sleeved cotton-knit shirt that buttoned partway down the front and a white sweater. Stephen carefully put on the shirt with some effort, moving slowly, trying not to strain his shoulder that still felt tender. The shirt fit him perfectly.

"Now for the sweater," said James who assisted Stephen after watching the difficulty he had putting on the shirt. Stephen gradually pulled the wool sweater down below his waist. James looked satisfied with the way it fit. "There. How does that feel?"

"Soft and warm," said Stephen. "Thanks."

"Are you hungry? Can I get you something to eat?" inquired James.

"Yes. I'd like something now," Stephen answered slowly.

James headed for the door. "I'll get something from the kitchen."

Pastor Rich leaned forward in the chair. "I'm glad you have an appetite. That's a good sign."

Stephen looked at Pastor Rich inquisitively. "How long have I been here?"

Rich replied, "We found you late yesterday afternoon not far from here. You were alone, lying in a field. Based on your condition, you obviously had been attacked. Do you remember anything that happened to you?"

Stephen reflected on the previous day's events as best he could. At the moment, it all seemed like a half-forgotten nightmare. "I was on a hiking trip and was supposed to get to a bed and breakfast further down the road, but I decided to camp out instead. I laid down to rest, and the next thing I knew, two faces appeared out of nowhere. That's the last thing I remember."

"Can you recollect what they looked like? Any details? Words spoken?" asked Rich hopefully.

"Some things I do. It all happened so fast. It's hard to explain. It's like trying to remember individual snapshots instead of the whole movie. Maybe I'll remember more later after I've rested."

"I inspected the area and found nothing nearby. No personal belongings, no supplies of any kind."

"I guess they took everything." Stephen paused to weigh the gravity of his situation. "I'll need to get a new passport, IDs, cash, a jacket, camping gear. What a predicament."

Pastor Rich smiled reassuringly. "No need to worry about all that for right now. Let's concentrate on getting you feeling better." Rich leaned forward using a more serious tone. "Stephen, I wanted you to know that we contacted the authorities yesterday to report this incident. Other hikers and local residents need to be on guard and take extra precautions. Whoever did this might still be in the area."

Stephen had not thought about the two men still being around or possibly coming back. That was a bit unnerving. He became all the more appreciative for sleeping inside behind locked doors at night.

"On Monday, I will make arrangements for you to make a police report. You will get a copy of that for your records. Then I will drive you to the Canadian embassy in Edinburgh so you can get a new passport." He paused to let Stephen process his thoughts. He knew it was a lot to think about at one time, and Stephen still looked exhausted.

Although somewhat distraught, Stephen sat in awe of the pastor's kindness. It was such a relief to have someone think this through for him when he felt so unraveled. He smiled. "Thank you."

"One more thing. When you feel up to it, you are welcome to use our Internet to contact your credit card companies and notify friends or relatives so they know what happened and where you are staying. There's an office at the end of the hall. We can log you in to the system."

"That's perfect. I couldn't ask for more," Stephen said, heaving a sigh of relief. He was feeling less tense and more at home by the minute.

At that moment, James returned with a tray of hot soup and a slice of bread. "This should be good for starters. If you want more, there's plenty. If you feel like something more substantial later on, just ask. The bathroom is the first door down the hall on the right, and the kitchen is at the end of the hall, straight ahead. Just so you know."

Stephen looked curiously at James. "Excuse me, but you sound American. I was just wondering how you ended up working here?"

"My parents were Scottish missionaries here in this area before I was born. After ministering for about ten years, my father was encouraged to start a church in a rural part of New York with the help of a good friend of his. He agreed, so my parents moved to the states. I was born two years later. As I grew up and learned more about my father's work in Scotland, I began to feel called to come here to discover my roots, you might say. After a few months, I met Rich and his wife, and together we founded this mission house."

Stephen felt encouraged to see how God had led someone to fulfill a calling. He still hoped to find his own new destiny. "That's quite a story. You are obviously quite committed to your cause."

James smiled and nodded. "Now, if you will excuse us, Rich and I have some other work to do. Enjoy your lunch." The two of them exited the room and headed for the kitchen to assist Joyce and the staff with some cleanup.

Stephen reached for the bowl and stirred up the hot soup to determine what kind it was. It was a beef stew, loaded with carrots, potatoes, and onions. He began to eat the soup with gusto. It tasted as delicious as it smelled. Up until now, he had not realized just how hungry he was. The bread was freshly baked and hot, straight out of the oven. Stephen dipped the edge of the bread in the soup and ate it. Gradually, he felt more awake and eventually satiated. After placing the empty bowl and spoon back on the tray by the bedside table, he leaned up against the wall, adjusting the pillow behind him.

He had a fairly good view of the window now from this vantage point and took some time to admire the flowers just outside. He made a mental note to go out there at some point and look around.

Glancing about the room, he saw that it was immaculate, almost as if it had never been used before. The pristine walls were painted a pale blue with crown molding painted white. A pale blue rug, the same shade as the walls, lay beside the bed. Everything matched. Someone had taken some time and effort to decorate this place. Eventually, his body reminded him that he was still in the mending process so he laid down again, covering himself with the wool blankets. He sensed a deep warmth, inside and out, all the way down to his very bones, and it felt marvelous.

Pastor Rich returned about a half hour later to find Stephen stretched out, eyes open. "Stephen, tomorrow is Sunday. There's a church here off the main corridor. We have services at ten o'clock. Would you like to join us?"

"Yes, I'd like that. I might need to take my time getting down there." Pastor Rich assured him there was no rush and that someone would help him if need arose.

"Do you think you would like to join us for dinner this evening?" inquired Rich.

Stephen nodded. "Yes. Definitely."

Pastor Rich smiled. "You rest for now. I'll be back around five thirty." He walked out, quietly closing the door behind him.

Chapter 4

Several hours later, Stephen awoke to the sound of Pastor Rich knocking gently on the bedroom door. "Time for dinner. Can you get up on your own?"

"I'm going to try," said Stephen. He still felt a bit stiff and sore from the ordeal, but at least the room wasn't spinning anymore. He got to his feet, stretched, and the two of them headed down the hall.

Rich was pleased to see Stephen walk unaided. He looked stronger than the day before. "I'm glad you're feeling better this evening. There's a guest staying here that is about your age. I think you would enjoy meeting him. His name is Andrew. He'll be joining us for dinner this evening, so you'll get a chance to meet him."

Turning the corner, Stephen walked into an enormous room with eight long wooden tables and wooden chairs. Each table could seat about a dozen people. One of the tables was fully set with a red tablecloth, linen napkins, water glasses, utensils, and plain white china plates. A glass vase with an arrangement of blue wildflowers, the same kind as in Stephen's room, stood in the middle of the table.

Glancing around, Stephen noticed the large room boasted a high ceiling with exposed wooden beams, a brick fireplace at one end with two sofas, a large, rectangular coffee table, and a chair positioned in front of it, and a large window at the other end of the room overlooking the garden with a stone patio.

Awed by the spaciousness and grandeur of the room, Stephen turned his attention again towards the massive fireplace with its raised brick hearth, high enough to sit on with ease. A thick, wooden mantle ran across the entire length of the fireplace. On this beam, Stephen noticed several framed, group portraits and a large ceramic sculpture of Christ sitting with some children.

On either side of the fireplace stood built-in bookcases over six feet high and about fifteen feet wide, giving the impression that the lounge served not only as a gathering place for good conversation, but also doubled as a rather majestic library. Upon examining the collection more closely, Stephen noted dozens of books on theology, religious quarterlies, a King James Bible, the history of Scotland, some children's books, and various literary classics.

Looking straight up, Stephen almost felt for a moment like he had been transported back to Yellowstone National Park where he had taken a break from hiking at the Old Faithful Inn with its open beams and cathedral ceiling. The lounge, covering about a thousand square feet with its red carpet spread out in the center, was impressive to say the least. A large framed poster hung on one wall that read: "Give thanks to the Lord for He is good. His steadfast love endures forever." Underneath was written 1 Chronicles 16:34.

At this point, he began to distinguish various aromas wafting their way into the dining hall from the kitchen. Pastor Rich gestured to one of the dining room chairs, and Stephen sat down.

A few minutes later, others joined them, including James and two small boys who ran to meet their father, hugged him, and sat down on either side of him.

"Stephen, these are my two boys, Eric and Mark." Eric waved. Mark nodded his head in greeting.

Eric leaned forward and looked at Stephen more closely. "You're the man we found yesterday. I'm glad you're not dead. You looked awful."

Pastor Rich looked sternly at his son. "Eric," his father said firmly. "Would you like to think about what you just said?"

Eric looked apologetic. "Did I say something wrong?"

His father nodded. Placing an arm around his son's shoulder, Rich leaned over and asked very softly, "Do you think you can figure out what it was?"

Eric looked pensive for a moment, thinking about each of his three statements. "Was it the last part? I didn't mean it in a bad way. Honest."

His father hugged him reassuringly. "I know, son. Just make sure that all your comments are kind ones."

Eric looked over at Stephen. "I'm sorry. You look better now, and I really am glad you're not dead."

Stephen laughed. "Thanks, Eric. I am too."

Mark looked at Stephen and proudly announced, "I set the table this evening."

"And you did a fine job of it. Everything is in its place," said Stephen.

Mark smiled. "Mom taught us how to do it."

His father kissed Mark on the top of the head. "Mark always offers to assist, especially around mealtime. He is a tremendous help to his mother and me."

Eric tugged at his father's shirt. "I helped too."

His father put his arm around Eric's shoulder again. "Yes, you did. Look, Mom put the flowers you picked on the table. Don't they look lovely? She wants to show them off because they're so pretty and extra pretty because you picked them." Eric sat up straighter, smiled, and hugged his father again.

Rich glanced at them both. "Did you boys wash your hands before you sat down?" In response, they both held up two sets of clean hands for him to inspect. "Excellent. Thank you."

The kitchen door opened, and Joyce entered the dining hall with a large baking dish of shepherd's pie followed by another woman in a long white apron who carried several baskets of bread. Another woman, middle-aged, followed her with bowls of vegetables. Next, a young girl with deep-set green eyes, blond hair cascading down past her shoulders, brought in some pitchers of water. Stephen stared at her for a moment, swallowed hard, took in a deep breath, and diverted his eyes toward his dinner plate. Her face seemed to glow like the way a stained-glass window is illuminated from behind by the sun. She looked at Stephen and grinned, poured him a glass of water, set the pitcher down, and returned to the kitchen.

Stephen stared at her as she walked away and then turned to Pastor Rich. "Who's that?"

Rich spread his linen napkin on his lap and then turned his full attention toward Stephen. "Her name is Kenzy. It means 'fair one.'"

Stephen looked back in the direction of the kitchen. "The name suits her."

Pastor Rich smiled. "She is one of our volunteers. She comes here a few days each week. I'll introduce you to her when she comes back to join us."

Stephen looked pleasantly surprised, barely containing his enthusiasm. "She's joining us for dinner?"

Rich nodded. "All the volunteers and guests join us for dinner. By the way, after we finish eating, if you feel up to it, let's go to the office so you can go online and make contacts to the credit card companies and your family."

"You're right. I really should do that tonight," said Stephen who was actually at that moment thinking more about Kenzy, whose green eyes and blond hair had imprinted an indelible image in his mind.

A few minutes later, Joyce, Kenzy, the two other volunteers, and another guest sat down at the table. Pastor James asked everyone to join hands and bowed his head to lead the evening prayer. "Lord, please bless this meal and bless us in your service. Tonight, Lord, we ask your special blessing on Stephen for his full recovery. Thank you for your provisions and your amazing love for us all. Amen." The clinking of glasses and utensils commenced as the water pitchers exchanged hands, servings were spooned out, and food was passed around the table.

Stephen looked intently at Kenzy and then at Pastor Rich who immediately took his cue. "Kenzy, I don't think you have met Stephen LeBlanc. He is our new guest. He arrived yesterday."

Kenzy smiled at Stephen and said, "Hello. It's good to meet you." Her voice sounded delicate like the soothing resonance of harp strings playing a perfect chord drifting effortlessly on scented air. At that moment, the last few remnants of Stephen's pain floated somewhere off into oblivion. He answered simply, "Good to meet you too."

Joyce introduced herself and asked him how he felt. "Actually, I feel much better and quite at home here. Thank you."

Joyce smiled at Stephen. "We're glad you are here with us. You stay as long as you need." A plate of hot raisin bread was passed to Stephen, and he took a slice as he waited for the shepherd's pie to come his way.

One of the volunteers seated at the other end of the table, a woman named Emily, sat watching Rich's two boys. "Pastor, those are two of the nicest kids I've ever known. Sometimes I wish I had a few kids of my own."

Emily had retired from the business world after working thirty-five years as an executive secretary. At the mission, she volunteered to do cleaning and cooking each week. She had never married but loved interacting with all the children who passed through the mission. She taught Bible class one day each week, which Eric and Mark attended.

Rich beamed with pride looking at each of the boys. "They are wonderful, Emily. Joyce and I treasure them. But you know, scripture says that women who have no children are actually the mothers of all children. That's the message gleaned from Isaiah 54:1 I believe."

Emily's eyes widened. "Oh my. All children. All the children of the world." She reflected on the magnitude of the statement. "That's a lovely sentiment, and I'm sure it's intended as a blessing, but at the same time, I am glad I don't have to do all that laundry." Joyce burst out laughing and other women joined in with similar comments in full agreement.

Across the table from Stephen, a young man sat conversing with James. The man looked about Stephen's age, somewhere around twenty-five. He had dark hair, almost shoulder length, and was quite muscular. He smiled.

"Good evening, Stephen. I'm Andrew." He reached across the table and shook Stephen's hand with a strong grip. "I'm a guest here too. I just got here last night. Glad you could join us."

Andrew exuded a sense of independence and an air of confidence in every word he spoke. Although he seemed to command the attention of others, he delighted in hearing about their interests and escapades. Even though he was a new guest, he obviously had already befriended everyone around him. While he was quite amiable, Stephen somehow sensed that if Andrew had to defend himself, he would prove to be a very formidable adversary. From the look of his biceps, Stephen mused that this guest probably enjoyed bench-pressing cars as a hobby.

Andrew finished fixing his dinner plate as the last of the food was passed around. "So, Stephen. What do you enjoy doing? Fishing? Golf? Hiking?"

Stephen looked up somewhat amazed. "Actually, I like all of those things." It was as if Andrew intuitively knew how he spent his time. "I was on a hiking trip when all my camping gear was stolen so that won't be an option for now. In the meantime, are there places around here to go fishing and play golf?"

Andrew nodded. "There's a great fishing spot about two miles from here full of salmon. I caught a six pounder there last week. I couldn't believe it. The area is absolutely beautiful, serene." He paused and looked across the room smiling, as if the entire scene had manifested itself on the wall. "In fact, I'd like to build a house there someday. The golf course is about five miles the other way. Eighteen holes. Gorgeous scenery. The course offers some real challenges." He paused to take a bite of bread, savoring it. "Delicious bread, Joyce."

She smiled. "Thank you, Andrew. I'm glad you're enjoying it."

Turning to Stephen, he said, "If you like, you can come fishing with me on Tuesday. I have an extra fishing pole. I had originally planned to spend the day alone, but it would be nice to have some company."

Stephen nodded. "That sounds wonderful. I'd like that."

Stephen began cutting into the shepherd's pie, tasting its wonderful flavor, and trying to figure out how Joyce could take something so simple and turn it into something so delicious. It was just as good as the beef stew he ate for lunch. He looked at the other end of the table at Kenzy who was chatting with one of the other volunteers. She glanced up at Stephen, saw him looking her way, and smiled at him. He returned the smile and then turned his glance again toward Andrew.

"Andrew, where are you from?"

Andrew took a long drink of water and set down the glass. "America. Philadelphia area." Stephen wondered what brought him this far from home. Somehow Andrew anticipated his next question. "I liked the idea of working overseas, so my company transferred me to their branch in Glasgow. I was working there for a year, then I came here because, well, I needed to get away, far away, for a couple months. It's complicated. I really was due for a change."

Stephen sensed there was more to this story than Andrew was telling but decided not to question him further. Stephen looked up from his plate. "I know how you feel. I quit my job a year ago looking for a change. I don't know what lies in store for me, but it has to be better than the mess I walked away from."

Pastor James looked at Stephen. "I'm sure God has a plan. He always does."

About twenty minutes after dinner, the dishes had been cleared. Hospitable as always, Joyce had served another round of coffee which served as a catalyst for additional conversation.

Leaning back in his chair, after a full meal, Andrew felt relaxed as the philosophical side of his character emerged. "Stephen, you enjoy hiking, right?" Stephen nodded. "Here's a question for you. What do you think is more important: the journey or the destination?"

Stephen reflected a moment. "If you are talking about life's journey and destination, both are significant. Ultimately, I would have to say the destination. After all, if you don't know where you are headed or don't care where you are going, what difference does it make where the journey takes you? The journey becomes meaningless, nothing but aimless wandering. On the other hand, for someone who just wants to get away for a couple weeks, that could be someone's definition of a vacation."

Rich smiled. "Just like when we found you."

Stephen laughed. "I must have just looked so attractive lying there. I guess that didn't look much like a vacation, did it?"

Andrew and Rich smiled. In a more serious tone, Pastor Rich observed, "I would have to agree with your initial conclusion, Stephen. I think anyone who says the destination has no meaning is not headed toward heaven. Sadly, that could cause one to conclude that life is meaningless, not just the idea of a destination." The others nodded in agreement.

Eric was still seated next to his dad but decided it was time to introduce himself to Andrew. Eric, who was always quite gregarious, pulled up an extra chair next to Andrew and sat down. "I'm Eric. I live here. Do you like cars?"

Andrew smiled down at the five-year-old. "Yes, I do. I have a car. It's green."

Eric's eyes widened. "A real car, like Dad's. Someday I want a real car too. My toy car is green. It's one of my favorite things. It can go really fast on the kitchen floor, but Mom always tells me to play with it outside on the patio." Andrew was intrigued by the child's openness and outgoing mannerisms.

Eric stood on top of the chair, looking at Andrew directly in the eyes. "Andrew, are you strong? Do you have muscles?"

Andrew looked surprised and laughed. He had not anticipated that question. "I guess so."

Eric looked delighted. "Good. Would you throw me up in the air and catch me? Please." Eric's big dark eyes were trusting and hopeful.

Andrew looked around. "Let's move into the other room away from the tables and chairs." Eric climbed down and trotted into the spacious lounge area.

Standing in an open space void of furniture, Andrew bent down and picked up Eric easily almost as if he were weightless. "OK, pal. Are you ready? Here we go!" He tossed Eric into the air. He squealed with delight, arms outstretched, as he sailed through the air and Andrew caught him. Eric's father watched, feeling grateful that the lounge area had a twenty-foot ceiling.

"Again, again," Eric shouted. Andrew threw him up in the air, and Eric laughed, enjoying his momentary flight. Soaring through the air a little higher the third time, Eric called out, "Look, Dad. I'm a bird. I can fly."

His father laughed. "Yes, I can see that."

After a few more tosses, Andrew said, "That's enough for tonight."

Eric somewhat reluctantly agreed and ran off to another part of the house to play with Mark.

Rich smiled at Andrew. "The kids both adore you. It's like you are part of the family."

Chapter 5

Sunday morning the kitchen came alive, bursting with clamor along with the smell of sizzling bacon, fried eggs, grilled sausages, homemade bread, and multiple pots of brewing coffee. As the women worked, they sang a verse or two from hymns. The boys set the table, carefully placing each item in its proper place. In the lounge area by the fireplace, the two pastors discussed the order of the morning service.

James sat looking rather agitated and perplexed. "Rich, I want to change the sermon for this morning. The Beatitudes offer great sermon material, but I don't think that's what the congregation needs. It's not what I need."

Rich looked at him curiously. "What are you talking about?"

James stood up and started pacing, while glancing about the room. "Do you ever think that what we do here really makes a difference? We are so remote, so isolated. We work with so few people. What impact do we have? In the grand and glorious scheme of things, does our work matter? Do we really help anyone? Do we give enough of ourselves?"

Rich stared at James. The two of them had worked together long enough that Rich could feel the tension in the air and his friend's need for reassurance. "James, do I need to remind you that you just helped save a man's life the other day? In the 'glorious scheme of things,' don't you think that matters? Isn't all life sacred to God even the life of just one man?"

James stopped pacing and looked at the floor, collecting his thoughts. He had allowed his emotions to cloud his judgment. He began forming a response in his mind but decided to let Rich continue speaking. It was time for the teacher to become a student again, at least for the time being.

Rich looked at him compassionately. "James, stop and think about why we started this mission in the first place. There was nothing here. Even people in remote villages have a right to hear the gospel and grow in faith."

James could hardly argue with that. "You're right. That is important, and I'm glad we were there to help Stephen. It's just that it seems so easy for us, for everyone, living out here almost in the middle of nothing. I've been comparing myself to other pastors with larger congregations and heavier responsibilities. I shouldn't have done that. I want to rewrite the sermon, but there isn't time."

Rich could feel his friend's tension rising. "What exactly is on your mind? What do you want to talk about?"

James took in a deep breath and sighed. "My own need to avoid complacency. I just somehow want to do more for God. I want to inspire everyone to do more for God. That's what I want to tell everyone this morning. The fact that all of us should do more for the Lord, since he did everything for us."

Rich stood up and put a hand on the pastor's shoulder. "James, I understand the feeling of desiring to do more, but at the same time, don't be overly hard on yourself. God doesn't call anyone to try and save the whole world. His son already did that."

James smiled and gave his friend a hug.

Rich looked him in the eyes. "James, whatever you want to say, pray about it and say it from your heart. Remember, James, our work is not without purpose. It just simply addresses a different set of needs due to our circumstances, but that does not make it insignificant."

"You're right. Thanks. I needed to hear that." James left for his office to work on his sermon revision.

Meanwhile, Andrew and Stephen sat conversing on the patio, looking out at the horizon as the dawn continued its gradual sweep over the mountains. The morning mist had gradually lifted, unveiling a tapestry of interwoven shades of green interspersed with patches of wildflowers of various colors. The contrasts were stunning. The air was chilly this morning, so Stephen was extra grateful for the knit shirt and wool sweater generously donated the day before.

Sipping a cup of hot coffee, Andrew pointed over to the right. "The golf course is in that direction, just a short five-mile drive. Just breathtaking, of course, with views of the Highlands in all directions. It's a fabulous place to spend the afternoon. Believe me, if you can't relax there, you can't relax anywhere. You can commune with God and nature at the same time."

Stephen nodded gazing at the Highlands. Having spent so many months hiking in the past few years, he understood exactly what Andrew meant. "I was just thinking of a verse from Psalms: In his hand are the depths of the earth, and the mountain peaks belong to him."

Andrew smiled. "Indeed, they do. And everything else besides." He paused admiring the landscape.

Since Eric had finished setting the table, he came out to the patio, noticed Andrew sitting in a metal chair, and climbed into his lap. Andrew gave him a little hug and smiled at him, thinking to himself: This kid is lots of things, but bashful is not one of them.

Eric smiled at Andrew. "I like sitting out here with you. It's pretty here. Sometimes I sit with my dad outside by the front door on the steps. I have a new airplane. Would you fly my airplane with me sometime?"

Andrew nodded. "Sure. We can do that."

Eric turned to look at Stephen and waved. "You can play too, Stephen, if you want. Someday I want to go up in a real plane." Eric glanced around the yard. "It's fun to come outside to play and run. I run faster now. Dad says I'm getting bigger. What do you like to do outside?"

"I like golf and fishing. Has your dad ever taken you fishing?" asked Andrew.

Eric shook his head. "Not yet. He said he will when I'm a bit bigger." Eric turned to look at Stephen. "Do you go fishing too?"

Stephen nodded. "Yes, I would like to go fishing here sometime."

Eric smiled. "Sounds good."

Eric turned his attention back to Andrew. "Our neighbors have sheep. Did you know that? They eat grass. They walk all over the meadow back there." Eric pointed over to the left. "Just the other side of that hill. Sometimes they get lost and end up on the road or in our back yard. I touched a sheep once. He was soft. I liked that. When I'm bigger, Dad says he'll let me hold one."

"I had an uncle who raised sheep," said Andrew, grinning at the boy.

Eric got excited. "In Scotland?"

"No, in America, in a place called Texas. That is a long way from here. My uncle let me hold his lambs and bottle-feed some of them. When you hold a lamb, you use both arms. It's not like holding a cat. You have to pick them up gently in both arms and put them down gently because you don't want to hurt them."

Eric smiled. "I'll try to remember." Eric could hear Mark talking inside. "I think I'll go in and see what Mark's doing. Bye. Bye, Stephen." Eric climbed down from Andrew's lap and ran into the dining hall.

Andrew smiled as he watched Eric run into the house. "He sure is a little firecracker, isn't he? Have you ever seen so much energy?"

Stephen laughed. "He's a sweet kid. I've liked getting to know him."

Andrew sat back in the chair. "So, Stephen, when did you start playing golf?"

Stephen reminisced about his first day on a golf course. "My dad first took me to a course when I was around twelve. We were vacationing in southern California and spent a week at a resort at Palm Springs. He paid for me to take some private lessons in the morning, and then in the afternoon, we had time to play nine holes before dinner. After that, I couldn't wait to play on other courses. It's been one of my favorite pastimes ever since. Those were good times with my father."

Stretching his legs out in front of him, Andrew took a swallow of hot coffee and sighed. "I have memories of playing golf in the states with my father too. We always enjoyed each other's company."

"Do you get to see him often?" Stephen asked.

Andrew got quiet for a moment, eyes fixed on the horizon. He sat up straight and poured some cream into the steaming hot coffee and watched the white substance silently explode, spreading out to the edges of the cup like a miniature atomic blast. He sat back in the chair, looking back out at the horizon.

"I'm afraid I can't see him anymore. I really wish I could, but he died about a month ago." Andrew paused and sighed. "He worked with me in Glasgow at the same company, as a matter of fact. He was going to teach me everything to work my way up to the top. He knew how to make money, and he knew how to manage people. He was showing me how to forge ahead. Unfortunately, those plans came to a sudden halt."

Stephen looked at him sympathetically. "I'm really sorry to hear that. It must be difficult."

Andrew sat quietly looking out across the panoramic view. "It feels like this back yard goes on forever. Sometimes I wish it did. I love the privacy here."

At that moment, James opened the patio door. "Gentlemen, breakfast is ready."

Once again, the table was laden with numerous plates of food and conversations were abundant. Mark looked up at his mother. "I love the way you fix roast lamb. I'm glad we don't just eat it at Easter time."

Joyce hugged Mark. "Thank you, dear. But you need to finish your breakfast first. We'll have lamb after Sunday services. I even have a special dessert prepared."

"What is it?" asked Mark with anticipation.

His mom smiled. "It's a surprise."

Mark squirmed with delight in his seat and turned toward his father. "Dad, don't forget you have to take me to soccer practice this week on Wednesday afternoon."

Rich looked at Mark. "I remember. We'll leave at twelve thirty."

Eric tugged at his mother's sleeve. "Did you make shortbread? You know I love shortbread. Do we have any?" asked Eric, his big eyes begging for a positive reply.

"Not today, Eric. But I will probably do more baking this weekend."

Eric looked a bit disappointed. From his perspective, next Saturday felt as far away as next Christmas.

"So, Stephen. How does that eye feel? I noticed the discoloration is clearing up quickly," said James.

"It doesn't ache anymore, and my shoulder is starting to loosen up. I must have landed on it when I got knocked out," said Stephen. Rich refilled Stephen's coffee cup and then his own. "Thanks, Rich. This coffee is wonderful."

"I think it's because of our well water. There's nothing added to it, just pure mountain water."

"Stephen, I put several changes of clothes in the dresser and some more shirts and sweaters in your closet," said James.

Stephen looked grateful. "I don't know what to say. That is so kind of you."

"Andrew is to thank for some of the donated items," said James, pointing in his direction.

At the other side of the table, Andrew was making a gesture indicating the length of a fish he had caught. "It was at least this long, and the bass was five pounds. That was good eating. I can't wait to get to the river this week."

"Andrew, James just told me you gave me some of your clothes. Thanks."

Andrew smiled. "No problem. I usually pack too much when I travel anyway."

The women chatted about family and friends. Kenzy smiled across the table at Stephen who kept hoping for a chance to talk with her in private.

Although he was eating with folks he barely knew, Stephen felt like he was dining at a family reunion. Kindnesses and courtesies overflowed everywhere.

At nine thirty, the table was cleared and the breakfast cleanup began. With so many volunteers, it took little time to put everything away. A few minutes before 10:00 a.m., church bells rang and everyone, with bibles in hand, walked into the sanctuary.

The brick church was simply furnished with wooden pews. At the front, a pulpit stood off to the right with two chairs a few feet away. The altar consisted of a table about four feet long. In the center was a wooden cross, a small floral arrangement, and two candlesticks, one on either side. On the wall above the altar, Stephen noticed a stained-glass window of Christ, the shepherd, with a lamb around his shoulders.

Joyce sat with her husband and the boys, who obviously had been taught how to behave in church. From the moment they stepped through the door, the tomfoolery and talkativeness stopped. Andrew joined Stephen in the middle of a pew in the front row. Sermon notes in hand, James took his place up front in a chair by the pulpit. One of the volunteers sat down at the piano and opened a hymnal. The other volunteers filed in behind Pastor Rich and his wife. In addition, about three dozen residents from neighboring villages also entered quietly and sat in the middle rows.

James stood up. "Pastor Rich, would you please come forward and lead us in singing 'Jesus Shall Reign'? That's number 235 in your hymnals."

Rich took his place in between the first two rows of pews and led the song with piano accompaniment. After some opening prayers, and reciting Psalm 23, the group sat down in anticipation of the scripture reading and sermon.

Pastor James stepped up to the pulpit. "Good morning. Please open your bibles and turn with me to the gospel of Luke, chapter 13, verses 23 and 24. Hear the words of Jesus." James paused a moment and began reading. "And someone said to him, 'Lord, will those who are saved be few?' And he answered them, 'Strive to enter in through the narrow door, for many I tell you will seek to enter and will not be able.'"

James looked out at his small, but attentive, congregation. "Today's sermon is entitled 'Complacency Is Not an Option.' As Christians, we all embrace Christ's command to love others. This love is the very foundation of this mission house, and Christ is the cornerstone. However, we must be on guard. This love we have for others, this gift of God's Holy Spirit, must never be taken for granted and never watered down to a mere feeling, an emotion that ceases to display itself in concrete actions and uplifting words. It is why we must daily, conscientiously strive to enter in through the narrow door: the door of obedience, the door of repentance, the door of self-sacrifice, the door of service.

"The word 'service' and variations of this word appear more than one thousand times in the New Testament alone. That should give you some idea how seriously the Lord takes the concept of loyal service, actions that are demonstrations of loving God and loving one's neighbor. Jesus referred to these as the two greatest commandments.

"It is so easy to look at a problem in society like homelessness, hunger, or those victimized by senseless crime and think: Somebody ought to do something. My friends, that somebody is you, and in saying that, I include myself. In the book of 1 Corinthians, chapter 12, verse 27, we read, 'All of you together are Christ's body, and each of you is a part of it.' My friends, please do not take these words lightly as mere metaphors. As Christ's body, we are to be imitators of Christ. As such we must serve others in love as he served us.

"As servants, we must offer God our hands to help wherever needed and our feet to take us wherever he calls us to go. We must always stand ready to offer God all we have. Complacency is not an option. We have no right to find our salvation in Christ only then to sit back passively, ignore his great commission to share the message of salvation, disregard the suffering of others, and wait comfortably for the Second Coming. If we do, our inaction makes us as guilty as those who initiated the troubles in society in the first place, and at the same time, we deny the law of love established by Christ Jesus."

James paused and looked into the eyes of those seated. He continued. "Please do not regard your role as a servant as insignificant. You are a unique individual. In all of human history, there will be only one of you. No one else in history will ever have your exact same sphere of influence for doing good. No one else will ever have your set of contacts consisting of your neighbors, your friends, your business associates, your church, and your family. You are the only person who can fulfill your role, a role that God has appointed for this particular place and time, so play your part well and serve your king.

"My friends, always remember, the Lord loves each of us up close and personal, not long distance. We are not afterthoughts. We are the crowning glory of his creation, made in his image, loved and cherished above all else. This is why our God from the beginning of time decided he would rather die than live without us and he loves us still. God hears our daily petitions. He knows our needs before we even ask. He feels empathy with our struggles and weaknesses and blesses us with his strength. In fact, he identifies so strongly with each of us that in Matthew 25:40 he says, 'Whatever you did to the least of these my brethren you have done unto me.' Therefore, we must bless our neighbors in need and offer them our love and strength. By loving our neighbors, we love Christ.

"A man once asked Jesus, 'Who is my neighbor?' The Lord's answer was the Parable of the Good Samaritan. In that story, there were those who passed by the injured man in the road. Those who ignored him had plans; more accurately, they had excuses. Only one traveler made that innocent victim a top priority. Only one cared about the suffering of another. Only one did anything about it. Learn from this example. Never let your own agenda outweigh the need of someone in crisis. After all, if the situation were reversed, you would want someone to do the same for you.

"As his servants and his followers, Jesus calls us by name. John 10:3 reads, 'The sheep shall hear his voice and he calls his own sheep by name and leads them out.' What does it mean that he 'leads them out?' Where are we being led? To a spiritual place of understanding where we grow closer to God's love? Yes. To a place of inner peace and hope for our souls? Definitely. But if we fully interpret this verse, in light of other scriptures, we must acknowledge that he also leads us to places of service, places to evangelize others with the gospel, places to alleviate suffering, and places where we ourselves might suffer for others for his name's sake.

"The Lord said, 'I send you out as sheep among wolves.' These wolves come in many forms of evil and deception: liars, tempters, thieves, the politically corrupt, the power hungry, and those who persecute us and directly attempt to destroy our faith and at times perhaps even our very lives. In the midst of trials, the Lord has promised to walk with us. In Hebrews 13:5, to those who follow him, he vows, 'I will never leave you, nor forsake you.' He will lead us through times of oppression when they come. Of course, ultimately, he will lead us to our final destination: the kingdom of heaven.

"Some of you may be thinking, 'Why worry about service? Why worry about good deeds? Doesn't scripture say we are saved by faith?' The key issue is a full understanding of the word 'faith.' Ephesians 2:8 addresses that issue. 'For by grace you have been saved through faith.' Let's continue reading with verse nine which reads 'not by works so that no one can boast.' This allows each believer to acknowledge Christ's work of redemption, our means of salvation. At the same time, this glorifies the Lord for his sacrifice on the cross. This verse and others remind us that we can never buy our way into heaven with our good deeds, but let's examine the subject further. Turn with me in your bibles to James 2:26. This passage says, 'For the body apart from the spirit is dead so faith apart from works is dead.' What does faith look like when it has no works? Selfish, fruitless, meaningless, lifeless. Simply put, good deeds are a demonstration of a genuine faith that leads one to salvation.

"On the last day, Jesus will say to some, 'Welcome to my Father's kingdom.' To others he will say, 'I never knew you.' Why will he tell some that he does not know them? It is because they did not follow their shepherd's voice when he called them by name. It is because they did not know Jesus intimately through prayer and service to others as Jesus commanded and demonstrated himself countless times. How easy it is to focus on self and let the world turn and confront its own problems. What kind of service is that? What demonstration of love is that? If we have genuine faith, we love. If we love, we obey. If we obey, we serve. If you truly love God, put your trust in the mercies of Jesus, and serve others, at the end of life, the Lord will personally welcome you to the Father's kingdom with the words 'Well done, good and faithful servant.'

"In closing, if anyone feels a need for strength to continue serving the Lord, read Psalm 121:1–2. 'I lift up my eyes unto the hills. From where does my help come? My help comes from the Lord, the maker of heaven and earth.' King David knew pagan practices took place in those hills, so he looked beyond the hills, to the heavens for he knew that beyond the heavens he would find the kingdom of God and the Lord, the source of his help. We would do well to do likewise.

"Let us pray. Lord God, we thank you for the call to serve you. Keep us ever mindful of the needs of others. With the guidance of your Holy Spirit, direct our minds and actions for your glory and help us to inspire others to true faith in you. In Jesus's name, Amen."

Stephen sat quietly reflecting on the sermon. He could identify with the man in the parable who was set upon by thieves. He looked over at Pastor Rich. The depth of his compassion for a total stranger was indeed inspiring. Rich had cleaned his wounds and stayed up all night in prayer. Stephen looked up at James and remembered how he had carried him down the path into the mission and brought him clothes and food. He thought about Andrew giving away his clothes to someone he had just met. He thought of Joyce's effort to cook meals for him. All four of them were Good Samaritans. God had truly been looking out for him. Stephen had asked for nothing and yet had received everything he needed. He sat in silence, feeling humbled.

As the collection plate was passed, Stephen regretted having nothing to give, but then again, after the robbery, he had no choice.

James looked out at the congregation and smiled. "Let us turn our hymnbooks to number 234, 'Be Thou My Vision.'" The pianist returned to the front and began to play. Communion followed and then another hymn and some closing prayers. At that point, the volunteers and guests once more headed for the kitchen and dining hall.

Within minutes, Joyce brought out the promised roast lamb on a large platter and placed it in the middle of the table. The seasonings from the meat permeated the room. Mark swayed in his chair in total delight. As before, the volunteers carried out side dishes and baked bread.

Rich asked everyone to join hands and bow their heads. "Lord, I thank you for the love around this table. I thank you that we can dine as friends and family. I thank you for your mercy that refreshes us each morning. Bless our meal and keep us mindful of the needs of others as your servants. Amen."

"James, that was a fabulous sermon. It gave me lots to think about," said Andrew. "'Never let your own agenda outweigh the need of someone in crisis.' I am going to remember that."

James smiled and passed a huge platter of lamb in his direction. Andrew took a slice and passed it on to Joyce.

"So, Andrew, is the fishing trip still on for Tuesday?" asked Stephen.

Carving into the slice of lamb, Andrew looked up. "Absolutely. I wouldn't want to miss it."

Eric put down his fork, looked over in Andrew's direction, and grinned, whispering, "I know a secret. I know a secret."

His mother glared at him. "Eric, hush. Eat your food." Joyce looked at Andrew who continued discussing the fishing trip with Stephen. She wasn't sure if Andrew had heard Eric's remark or not.

Rich passed a bowl around with another helping of potatoes. "James, I think in two weeks we will have a group from Edinburgh here, Church of Scotland. There will be about thirty of them. They'll want to stay for three days, maybe four. The pastor is going to contact me in a couple of days to make final arrangements."

James looked pleased. "Wonderful. If this keeps up, we are going to need another pastor here to help us out. Are you going to lead the lectures and study groups, or should I?"

Rich thought a moment. "Let's see if we can each do half. That way our individual schedules won't change too much."

James agreed.

At the end of the meal, Joyce gestured for Mark and Eric to go to the kitchen. The boys ran through the kitchen door smiling and laughing. Joyce followed them. A moment later, she reappeared carrying a birthday cake, covered with chocolate frosting, lit with candles around the edges. In the middle of the cake was the name "Andrew" in white icing with a white heart underneath it. Joyce placed the cake in front of Andrew who looked shocked. Everyone joined in with a rousing chorus of "Happy Birthday."

Andrew stared at all of them. "How did you ever find out?"

Rich smiled. "Remember when you registered? Writing down your birthdate was an option. You filled in the space."

"I lit the candles," said Mark.

"I made the heart," shouted Eric.

Andrew looked a bit sentimental. "You guys. Honestly. This is too much. Thank you, all. I haven't had a surprise birthday in years."

Eric, with visions of chocolate cake slices swirling through his mind, pleaded, "Come on. Make a wish."

Andrew paused. "Yes. There is something I'd like to wish for." After a moment, he blew out the candles.

Joyce proceeded to cut the cake and pass it around.

Dying of curiosity, Eric put his arm around Andrew's neck and whispered, "What did you wish for?"

Andrew grinned at him. "It's a secret."

Chapter 6

As promised, Monday morning after breakfast, Rich had a local police officer come by the mission so Stephen could give his official statement concerning the assault and robbery. He explained in detail that he had entered the country a week ago, flying from the international airport in Quebec City to Edinburgh. From there, he had taken a bus about forty miles to a village. He was one of only six passengers on the bus, and he was certain that the men he encountered later were not traveling with him. After arriving at the village, he had hiked into the Highlands to begin his camping trip, averaging about five to ten miles a day.

One day, when it had poured rain, Stephen hitched a ride from a young man of about twenty who was headed west, but other than that, he had walked. Aside from buying some supplies, and the other incidents mentioned, he had not made contact with anyone, except for the assailants of course, until he met Rich and James at the mission. Rich verified the exact location, time, and date where he had found Stephen, along with the dreadful circumstances.

In addition, Stephen provided a list of all the personal items that were stolen and their approximate value. The officer also questioned the two boys to corroborate the account and asked them if they had seen anyone else around or noticed anything suspicious. They had not.

While being asked about the two men who approached him, Stephen began remembering some of the details. Stephen's best guess was that both men were somewhere between thirty and thirty-five years old. Both men were Caucasians with dark hair, and one wore a green quilted jacket. One had called the other one Sam. Stephen also considered the idea that they might have located him due to the smoke from his campfire. Of course, being a foreigner and new to this area, he had to conclude that the two men did not know him personally. This was just a case of being at the right place at the wrong time, and therefore a random act of violence, not a premeditated crime.

The officer took detailed notes the entire time. Periodically, he would read back his statements to Stephen to confirm their accuracy. After finishing the notes on his laptop, he asked Rich if there was somewhere he could print out the report so Stephen could keep a copy. Rich led him down the hall to the office. A few minutes later, they returned, and the officer handed Stephen a copy of the report.

"Mr. LeBlanc, I want to thank you for your cooperation in this matter. It may indeed prove quite useful to our department. These two might have been involved in other crimes. I have already e-mailed my staff the details so they can begin processing this information. The investigation may lead to a match to the identity of these assailants."

Rich and Stephen thanked the officer for his time as he left. Rich turned to Stephen. "Now that you have your police report, let's get to the embassy. It's a long drive, so we should leave now."

Stephen grabbed his jacket from the closet and went out front with the pastor to the car. It was indeed a long drive to Edinburgh, but at least it was quite scenic. The day was overcast. About halfway to Edinburgh, rainclouds and fog threatened to cover the view, and a few minutes later, Rich and Stephen found themselves driving in a downpour.

"I know it might seem that this weather spoils the day, but of course, we need the rain and we get lots of it. That's why it's always so green around here," Rich commented.

"I don't mind rain as long as I'm not walking in it. Years ago, I was visiting some of my cousins in the states. They had experienced an extended drought. Their yard looked awful. All brown. One afternoon we cut across the yard to walk down to a main road to a convenience store. Honestly, walking across that lawn was like walking across a bowl of cornflakes. Dry and crunchy. Believe me, my cousins would have given anything to have had rain like this."

Upon arriving at the Canadian embassy, Stephen and Rich walked into the front office. Aside from office staff, they were the only two there. A secretary escorted Stephen to a back room where he began filling out paperwork to start the process of acquiring a new passport. He presented his police report to an embassy official who questioned him for about half an hour, photographed him, and told to sit in a waiting area.

"I can't believe how quickly they took care of that. I anticipated being here for hours," Rich said in amazement. About a half hour later, an embassy official handed Stephen a passport. He could not believe his eyes. He stared at the passport in pleasant disbelief, but he could not deny the reality of the document in his hands. He thanked the man and left with Rich.

By now it was after one o'clock in the afternoon. The sun had returned, and most of the clouds had moved on. "How about some lunch? I know a good restaurant that has a view of the city. It's actually on the roof of the National Museum of Scotland."

"You know the way, so lead on. I am getting hungry," Stephen responded.

"I think you will like this place. It's called Tower Restaurant. You can see the castle from there and a large part of downtown." Stephen followed Rich for a few blocks and entered the museum, taking the elevator to the top floor. After requesting a table by a window, the two sat down.

"What a magnificent view," said Stephen, who was glad Rich had brought his camera with him. This was his first time seeing the downtown area and the restaurant proved to be an outstanding vantage point for observation.

Rich pointed to the castle. "It dates back to the Middle Ages and survived a number of wars and sieges. The long street leading up to the castle is called the Royal Mile. It's a steep incline, but there are a number of interesting places along the way."

Rich handed Steven the camera. Grateful for the opportunity, Stephen turned sideways in his chair to frame some good photographs. From the vicinity of the castle, the two men could hear the sound of bagpipes, a time-honored tradition. Stephen snapped a few photos of the cityscape and castle, a regal structure that preserved the memory of the land's ancient heritage. Handing the camera back to

Rich, Stephen said, "Thanks. I'll pay you for those pictures when you get them printed. They will make a great souvenir." Rich smiled. "I'll take you by the Princes Street Fountain before we go so you can see it up close. It's quite remarkable."

A waiter presented them with menus that featured Scottish cuisine. Being a bit of a connoisseur where fish were concerned, Stephen ordered a fish entrée, a combination of haddock, potatoes, onions, and cream. If it turned out to be as flavorful as it sounded, he would tell Andrew about it. In the short time he had known Andrew, one thing Stephen knew for certain: Andrew loved finding new ways to cook fish. Stephen began to wonder if Joyce could cook a fish chowder of some sort for dinner. Rich also ordered haddock, but a different entrée served with bacon and sage.

About thirty minutes later, the two men sat dining and enjoying the view. "Today has actually turned into an adventure. This feels more like I am back on vacation," Stephen announced, reveling in the flavor of the fish, while delighting in the ambiance of the restaurant.

Rich smiled. "I'm glad life is slowly coming back to normal. You went through quite an ordeal."

Stephen reflected over the past few days and admired the magnificent view from their table. "It has been exhausting in a way, but I am so relieved that I have met all of you. I can't believe my good fortune. My luck changed overnight."

Rich looked up at him. "Stephen, it wasn't luck. It was providence."

"You're right. After all these blessings, I should throw the word 'luck' out of my vocabulary." They both laughed.

"Rich, do you think when we get back that I could help out in the kitchen tonight?"

"I suppose so, if you want to."

Stephen smiled. "I would like to do something to repay you a bit for your kindness, but I must confess I do have an ulterior motive."

Rich looked at him curiously. "What's that?"

Stephen smiled. "I'd like to spend some time with Kenzy. I haven't had a chance to talk with her or get to know her yet."

Rich smiled. "Ah, I see. Of course, you can help out in the kitchen. It will be an easy way for you two to get acquainted. She's a good person. I think you two would get along."

After lunch and a quick stop to photograph the Princes Street Fountain, driving back to the mission, Stephen asked Rich about Kenzy's interests. Rich thought for a moment. "She loves cooking as much as Joyce. In fact, last year she did most of the preparation for our Christmas dinner. That gave Joyce more free time to spend with me and the children. She also likes to play golf on her days off. She and her friends play at a local course."

Stephen was overjoyed. "Golf. Perfect. If our conversations go well, I can invite her to join me."

Stephen relaxed and spent some time admiring the scenery. "Rich, is Andrew planning on staying at the mission for a while like a week or two? I know we just met, but it seems like he and I could become good friends."

Rich paused trying to choose his words carefully. "Stephen, where Andrew is concerned, if you want to know something about him, you probably should ask him yourself. He has his reasons for staying with us just like everyone else does, but I can tell you he is a kind-hearted man, and a moral one. He would be a friend worth keeping, no doubt, but I wouldn't press him into talking about anything personal. That would be the best advice I could give you."

"He told me about his father passing not too long ago. I thought perhaps he came here for a while to unwind, to get a fresh perspective."

Rich made no immediate reply. He seemed preoccupied with his own thoughts and just kept his eyes on the road. On occasion he would glance off to his left to take in the view of the mountains. Finally, he said, "Andrew was very close to his father. That's a bond that was broken far too soon. Life can seem unfair at times, but scripture says, 'All things work together for good for those who love the Lord.'"

"We planned a fishing trip for tomorrow. That should be an opportunity to get better acquainted. That's a major interest we both share, that and golf."

"I'm glad you'll get a chance to know him better. He's an excellent fisherman and plays a good game of golf."

Stephen began to wonder how Rich knew so much about someone who had arrived at the mission the same time he had, just three days ago. Whatever else happened in Andrew's past, whatever reasons he had for staying at the mission, paled in comparison to the friendship the two of them were building. In some ways, Andrew reminded Stephen of his older brother, who had passed away a year ago. The two of them used to delight in fishing trips and golf games. Stephen reflected over the past few days. It had been as easy to talk with Andrew as it had been with his own brother. One more blessing from this unexpected adventure.

As they got closer to the mission, Stephen's thoughts returned to Kenzy. He could hardly wait to see her. By the time they arrived back at the mission, it was around four thirty. Hearing the volunteers talking in the kitchen, preparing dinner, Stephen walked in and saw Kenzy sitting at a table peeling potatoes. Stephen approached her. Her blond hair was tied in a long ponytail.

"Hi. Mind if I sit down?" She looked up and smiled. Looking into those green eyes was like discovering the beauty of a new star-studded galaxy at the other side of the cosmos.

"No, that's fine."

He watched her work for a moment. "Can I do anything to help?"

Her green eyes sparkled at him again, and she pointed to the sink. "You can help by washing some vegetables."

Since the sink was fairly close in proximity to where Kenzy was sitting, Stephen silently concluded that was a good place to work. Of course, at this point, he would have gladly scrubbed the entire kitchen floor on his hands and knees with a toothbrush if it meant being near her for any length of time.

Walking toward the sink, he rolled up his sleeves. Moving his hair over to one side, he bent over the sink and began the task of washing potatoes and turnips. He looked back at her as she worked. "So, Kenzy, how long have you worked here?"

"About two years," she said quietly.

"Have you volunteered at other places?" he asked.

"No, just here." Since the conversation lacked luster, he decided to go ahead and play his trump card, the real question he wanted to pose.

"Do you like to play any sports?" he asked. Thanks to his conversation with Rich, he already knew the answer to that question.

"Yes, I do. I enjoy swimming and playing golf when the weather is good. Do you play any sports?"

Stephen turned and smiled at her. "Yes, I love golf. Maybe we could go to the golf course together later on this week. How does that sound?"

Kenzy stopped working and smiled at him. "I'd like that," she said, her melodic voice sweetly drifting through the air.

At that moment, Stephen felt like his heart was shooting off more rockets than a Chinese New Year's celebration along the river in Shanghai. He smiled at Kenzy. "Perhaps Wednesday or Thursday this week?"

"Yes, that would be fine. Maybe you can give me some pointers to improve my game."

Stephen nodded. "Of course, I'd be glad to."

For the next half hour, they talked about various topics, including the first time each of them had played golf. Kenzy had learned from her father as well. She also asked him about his religious background. That question impressed Stephen. Kenzy was indeed a young woman of character. In all his dating experiences, Stephen could not recall one woman ever asking him questions about his faith. He realized he had probably been dating the wrong kind of girl until now. That revelation made him appreciate Kenzy all the more, so he answered every question she posed. He also told her about leaving his previous job, hoping God would give him a sense of direction. Kenzy acted intrigued by his honesty.

Around five thirty, the volunteers, staff, and guests all assembled again for dinner.

"Kenzy, would you like to sit next to me tonight?" asked Stephen hopefully.

She looked at him awestruck, as if seeing him for the first time. "I'd love to."

Chapter 7

Tuesday morning came, partly cloudy, but not a rain-cloud in sight, which was perfect weather for fishing. Andrew and Stephen sat in the dining room and finalized their plans for their fishing trip over breakfast.

Andrew spread some orange lemon marmalade on a large piece of bread. "I've got a car here, so I can load up the trunk with my gear and we take off whenever you're ready. You're going to love it," said Andrew. "You already have your fishing license, right?"

Stephen savored another strip of bacon. "Yes. I got one about a month ago. I'm looking forward to this. It's great to be outdoors. I don't feel up to hiking yet, so a fishing trip sounds ideal, a day to just sit and talk." The two ate for the next five minutes in silence. A hearty breakfast of this magnitude could not be taken for granted.

Finishing the last drop of a cup of hot tea and the last bite of bread, Andrew stood up. "Meet me out front in about twenty minutes. Joyce gave me free reign in the kitchen this morning to make some sandwiches, and she gave us some bottled juice so we don't have to interrupt our fishing to go elsewhere to eat."

"Fantastic. See you in twenty minutes."

The two men departed in different directions to their respective rooms. James had hung up a jacket in Stephen's closet along with a blue sweater and several more shirts. The generosity of this place proved delightfully shocking. He began wondering if he could figure out a way to repay their kindness somehow in a more substantial way than just helping out in the kitchen.

After straightening up the room and putting on his new brown, suede jacket, Stephen headed out front. Andrew was waiting for him in a green Honda. He smiled as Stephen slid into the front seat and said, "Let's go. This day is too good to waste a minute."

They drove off down a country road surrounded by green fields and the Highlands serving as the backdrop for this artistic masterpiece. Within minutes they arrived at a clearing in a wooded area with a wide stream. No one else was around. The place was so secluded that it almost seemed like the two of them were the only inhabitants in the whole world. If Eden ever had a fishing stream, it probably looked like this one.

Andrew pulled off the road about thirty yards from the riverbank. Opening up the trunk, he handed Stephen two fishing poles, two folding chairs, and a bag of sandwiches. The other items Andrew took himself, including a fishing net, his tackle box, and a container with ice, and headed down the embankment. Andrew had fished in this area a number of times, so he was quite familiar with the terrain. He had carefully selected an area that was flat with a gradual slope into the river. The water was so clear that from the shoreline you could see a foot down to the bottom.

Further out, the river became gradually deeper, with swifter currents.

About ten feet in from the shoreline, Andrew positioned his chair and sat down to prepare his pole. Opening up his tackle box, he selected a hook and lure and attached them to the line and then checked the setting on his reel and adjusted the line. He handed Stephen the tackle box. "Choose whatever lure and hook you like. I prefer to use roe for live bait when catching salmon. Some fishermen prefer to use cut up fish."

He handed Stephen the jar of roe, and he proceeded to put the bait on the end of the hook and attached one of the lures. "That's exactly what I use. I've always had good luck with roe," said Stephen who sat relaxed in his chair, pole ready in his hand.

"You can go first, and I'll stand ready with the net. It'll be easier that way. Later on, we can switch. If that shoulder is still giving you some trouble, I can cast off for you," said Andrew.

"That's probably a good idea. I don't want to aggravate it."

Andrew took the pole and cast off into the middle of the stream and handed Stephen the pole. Leaning forward, holding the pole in his left hand, Stephen prepared himself to stand in anticipation of a bite. Within a few minutes, Stephen's pole bent drastically, and he stood up to reel in his prize. As he brought the fish in closer to shore, Andrew got the net under the fish. Stephen estimated the catch was about four pounds in size. A beauty. After reeling in two more, Stephen set his pole down and assisted Andrew.

Casting off into the stream, Andrew stood ready, patient, but eager. Five minutes later, he began a fighting match with his prey as he coaxed it into shore. "I've got you. Come on. You're not getting away from me. Come on." The pole bent lower as the fish thrashed in the water in a futile attempt to free itself. "You can wrestle all you want, but you're not going anywhere. You're not going to win this fight. I've got you. You've been outsmarted. You've met your match. Come on. There we are." Andrew reeled in his first catch of the day. The fish was enormous. Stephen got the fish in the net, removed the hook, and placed it in the container with the others. After catching a few more, they took a break to enjoy the view.

"Andrew, I was watching how you talk to the fish as you reel them in. There's a legend about Saint Anthony of Padua. He would go down to the river and preach to the fish. Apparently, the fish were so intrigued with the sermon that they would line up in rows to listen. Maybe if you practice talking to fish enough you won't need your fishing pole anymore."

Andrew laughed and shook his head. He could hear the lighthearted sarcasm in his friend's voice. "I don't think they would head toward me if they knew I was going to eat them for dinner." Andrew gestured in front of him. "Didn't I tell you this was a fabulous spot? I could sit here all day."

They sat for some time in silence, taking in the view. At this point, about two hours had passed since they had left the mission. Stephen sat in the sun, legs stretched out, eyes closed, smiling, his face soaking up the precious rays.

Andrew looked over at Stephen who had a peaceful look on his face like he was about to enter paradise. "You could be the poster child for serenity."

Stephen laughed heartily. "I wouldn't mind as long as I don't have to move when I get photographed. This is so relaxing." Stephen reflected for a moment. "I was just remembering something John Muir, the naturalist, said: 'In every walk with nature one receives far more than he seeks.'"

Andrew meditated on those words for a moment. "That's absolutely true. I always come back rejuvenated. What's one of your favorite memories of a fishing trip?" Andrew asked.

Stephen, eyes still closed, began to dig up some childhood adventures. "I was just about to ask you the same question. The first time I went fishing with my dad I was about seven. We fished for salmon in Bonaventure. That's in Quebec. The water is so clear there. I was so little that my dad had to handle the pole. He held it, and I put my hands over his so I could feel the tug on the line. We caught a half dozen or so. My mother graciously cleaned and cooked several of them for dinner when we got home. That's one of my earliest memories."

Andrew looked across the stream to the embankment on the other side. His eyes followed a few birds that soared by. After being hidden a minute, surrounded and imprisoned by clouds, the sun broke free, its rays rejoicing, reflecting off the stream.

"My first fishing trip was with my dad too. We went to Lehigh River in Pennsylvania. That river is loaded with different kinds of bass and some catfish. I was six, so I fished with a bamboo pole. I quickly discovered that balance was an issue. When I got a bite, I had to lean back and then swing the pole over to the side to get the fish up on level ground where I could get at it. One time I caught a fish, it fell off the end of the line and somebody's dog came by and grabbed it and ran off with it. I guess the dog figured 'Finders keepers.' I was so upset. That was one of the first fish I had ever caught, and I didn't want to lose it, especially to a dog. Fortunately, the owner got the fish back for me, all in one piece. It makes me laugh when I think about it now."

Stephen sat up, opened the bag of sandwiches, and handed one to Andrew. Next, Stephen passed him a bottle of apple juice and opened one for himself. For the next ten minutes, the two sat eating in silence, connecting to the beauty of this hideaway.

"Stephen, how long do you plan to stay at the mission?"

Stephen set the bottle of juice down on the ground beside his feet. "I'm not sure. I managed to get my passport renewed yesterday. I still have to get credit cards reissued with new numbers. That will take some time. I'm using the mission as my mailing address for right now, so I guess I'll need to stay at least a few weeks. I also have to get some gear so I can hit the road again. Another problem is I don't even have an airline ticket now to get home. I canceled the ticket I had purchased originally because, of course, it was stolen along with everything else, so I'll need to get it reissued. Since I have a place to stay and my meals, there's no rush to get everything done immediately. Another problem is I have no cash."

"That is a lot to handle. What a relief that at least room and board are not a problem. I'll do what I can for you if you need some cash before you go. I can give you some of my extra fishing gear too if you want before you take off. I'm sure the pastors will also help out in other ways." Andrew paused. "I see you got the jacket."

Stephen looked at Andrew surprised. "This is your jacket?"

Andrew smiled. "No, it was my jacket. It's yours now. I figured we're about the same size, so my things should fit you."

"I can't thank you enough for this and the sweaters, but you didn't have to do that."

"That's all right. I wanted to." He took a long cool drink of juice.

Andrew watched the stream's current, how it flowed, unstoppable, splashing over the rocks in its path, creating swirls and eddies. The water seemed unrelenting, as if determined to reach some unseen goal. Although the rocks could redirect the water's movement for a moment, they could neither harness the stream's energy and power nor utterly impede its course.

"About an hour or so from here is another great place to fish: Loch Lomond. It's a fresh water lake. Great fishing," said Andrew.

"Maybe we can go there sometime. That's one place in Scotland I've never seen," said Stephen, taking another cool drink of juice.

Andrew sat up straighter, leaned forward, turned, and looked at his fishing partner. "Stephen, would you mind telling me about what happened on your camping trip, right before you got to the mission? I'm curious, that's all."

"Basically, I got robbed. Two men jumped me and took my things."

"Do you remember anything about them? What they looked like?"

Stephen wasn't sure why Andrew took an interest in those details but could see no reason not to tell him. "They were both tall, taller than I am at any rate. I found that out when they yanked me to my feet. One had dark hair and a green jacket. One man called the other 'Sam.'"

Andrew sat up a bit straighter and turned his head toward Stephen. "Sam? Did you hear a last name?"

"No, that's all. We struggled. They knocked me senseless, took my things, and left."

Andrew stood up and turned his chair facing Stephen directly. "I know you gave a police report, but have the authorities given you any follow up? Have they found any leads? Have they mentioned anything about an eyewitness or someone seeing something suspicious, anything that seemed out of place? A person, a car?"

Stephen looked curiously at Andrew. "No, I haven't heard anything from them yet. I'm sure they'll call if they find out anything."

Andrew sat looking pensive.

"Andrew, do you know something about this?"

Andrew looked back at the horizon. "I was just thinking about the fact that those men might be around here someplace." Andrew sat quietly for a moment. "What kind of a tent were you using for your trip?"

"It was a two-person dome tent."

"What color was it?"

"Red. Why do you ask?"

Andrew picked up another sandwich and tore it into two pieces. "Oh, just curious I guess."

Andrew's focus shifted. "So have you had a chance to chat with Kenzy? I see the way you two look at each other."

Stephen smiled, grateful for a change in the conversation. "Yes, as a matter of fact, I invited her to play golf tomorrow. I made a reservation at the course. James was kind to treat both of us to a round of golf, since I don't have funds yet. By the way, could you possibly drop us off? I have no other means of getting there."

Andrew nodded. "Yes, I can do that. I think I'll take a drive around the area tomorrow. You know, take a country drive. That should be relaxing. There's a few things around here I think I'll check out."

The two of them resumed fishing for several hours. By late afternoon, they decided to head back. Joyce put their fish in the freezer until such time as they decided to have some for dinner.

That evening, pastor Rich and James called a special meeting in the lounge for all volunteers and the two guests. James stood up, looking concerned, but composed.

"Good evening. I wanted to give you an update on some local news we have heard. Yesterday, two men robbed a convenience store in town about ten miles from here. The police strongly suspect that these men are hiding out somewhere in the area. So as a precautionary measure, we are asking that for at least the next two weeks all of you keep doors and windows locked. I know we are accustomed to visitors strolling in through the front doors, but for now, they will need to ring the bell and Joyce, Rich, or I will determine who enters."

James sat down, and Rich stood up to face the group. "Good evening, everyone. I wanted you to know that I share the same concerns as James regarding this matter. These two men may or may not be the same ones who attacked and robbed Stephen last Friday. That has not been determined. At any rate, be vigilant, and let us know if you see someone that seems out of place or anything you consider suspicious. Right now, we need a careful balance between openhandedness and our own safety." At these words, Rich's eyes expressed apprehension as he looked into the faces of his wife, the two boys, and then at Stephen.

"Your cooperation is greatly appreciated. We will keep you informed if we get any additional information. We plan on holding our weekly activities and worship services. Let us remember to pray for the safety of other guests who might be traveling this way."

The meeting broke up, and everyone began to disperse to different parts of the building.

Andrew turned to Stephen. "I'm glad we found out so we can keep our guard up. About tomorrow, I'll drop you and Kenzy off at the golf course around nine thirty. How about I pick you up around three o'clock? That way you can have the day together, play golf, eat lunch. How does that sound?"

"Perfect. I just realized I have no money to buy the two of us lunch."

Andrew got out his wallet and handed Stephen a small stack of bills. "Here. That will take care of lunch with some money left over." Stephen looked up at Andrew, speechless. "No need to thank me and no need to pay me back. Someday you can do something nice for somebody else. Is it a deal?"

Stephen nodded. "Yes, that's definitely a deal. I think I'll help Kenzy this evening, but I'll join you tomorrow for breakfast. How's that?"

Andrew smiled. "Sounds perfect."

Chapter 8

Wednesday morning after breakfast, as promised, Andrew dropped off Kenzy and Stephen at the golf course. Stephen thanked him and walked off with Kenzy to the clubhouse, a large brick structure on a knoll. They looked forward to teeing off, enjoying the outdoors, and facing the challenging aspects of the course. More importantly, it was their first date, one that would become the anniversary of their relationship. As Andrew watched the two of them get out of the car, he said, "Wait a minute. Let me get a picture." Andrew took his camera from the front seat and snapped a photo of the smiling couple with the golf course clubhouse in the background. Stephen waved as they walked toward the entrance. "Thanks, Andrew. See you this afternoon."

Andrew drove around the circular driveway and headed back down the country road. His intuition told him that the same men who robbed the store were indeed the same two men who had attacked Stephen. All he needed was some evidence to back up his theory. Since it was another sunny July day, he drove with the windows down, slowly, eyes checking out the landscape.

After driving about twenty minutes, Andrew slowed the car down to a crawl and then pulled over into the shoulder. There in front of him about a hundred yards away was a red domed tent, set up in an open field off the trail. Andrew took out his camera and snapped a photo, then turned the car around and headed back toward the village to report his findings.

The police building was quite small, with one desk in the front office. He walked up to the receptionist, who greeted him and asked how she could help.

"I have some information I'd like to share with one of your officers."

The receptionist gestured for him to take a seat and walked into the back room. A few minutes later, an officer emerged and opened the door to his office for Andrew.

"Please come in and sit down. I'm Daniel Stewart. What can I do for you?"

Andrew took a seat and looked behind him to double check that the door to the office was closed. "My name is Andrew Schafer. I'm staying at the mission outside of town. Earlier this week, you spoke with a young man named Stephen LeBlanc. He is an acquaintance of mine. Yesterday, we talked about the theft of his camping gear and money. He told me he had been sleeping in a red, two-person domed tent, which was stolen. Just now driving outside of town, I noticed a campsite with that same type of tent. I'm not saying that the thieves you're looking for are camping there, but I think someone should go check it out. After all, their motivation for stealing the tent and gear could have been to supply themselves with shelter."

The officer looked at Andrew rather intrigued. "That's an excellent point. They could be camping out. Red domed tent. That's a piece of information we did not get from Mr. LeBlanc when we questioned him. Actually, I don't think anyone asked him that specific question. That was an oversight on our part. Thank you for bringing this to our attention."

"I took a picture of the campsite," handing the officer his camera.

He examined the image. "Thank you. I will add this right now for our records." A few minutes later, after downloading the photo and typing in some details Andrew provided, he handed Andrew the camera back. "If you notice anything else or if Mr. LeBlanc remembers anything more about what happened, please contact us as soon as you can. In the meantime, I will send someone out to check out that campsite."

Andrew looked intently at the officer and leaned forward in the chair.

"Officer Stewart, there's something else I have to tell you. If these two men are indeed the ones I suspect they are, I want you to know that I was deputized to go after them. The men I am after committed felonies in the US as well as here in Great Britain. You can check that out with the police in Glasgow. They know me and can provide you with more details. I will gladly work with your force here to track them down and bring them to justice. I'll tell you more, if need be, but first we need to establish who is occupying that campsite."

Officer Stewart nodded, admiring the young man's courage.

"Just one more thing," said Andrew. "I would appreciate it if you would not tell anyone else that I came to see you, like Mr. LeBlanc or anyone at the mission and the part about being deputized. I'd rather tell them myself, if

I feel the time for that is right. The only person who really knows who I am and why I am here is Pastor Hunter, but please don't mention this meeting, not even to him."

Officer Stewart nodded. "Agreed."

Upon exiting the police building, Andrew strolled down the village streets, looking in shop windows at various displays and getting acquainted with the layout of stores and quaint restaurants. Toward one end of the village was a tavern with a large painted sign out front with the words "Crown and Shield." Andrew walked in, took a seat at a long wooden bar, and ordered a malt whiskey. The ceiling featured open beams with lights hanging from them. Over the bar to the right and left were rows of bottles. A Scottish family crest with the name McTavish hung in the center. A deer head was mounted along a back wall. Various framed photos of Scotland as well as some famous golfers lined the other walls. In the open area adjacent to the bar, two billiard tables were set up by the windows.

About fifteen minutes later, as Andrew sat there sipping his drink, two men walked in and sat down at a table about fifteen feet away. He turned to get a look at them and almost lost his breath for a moment. He stood up, walked to the opposite end of the bar, motioned to the bartender, paid his tab, and headed for the back door. He walked behind buildings for about thirty yards and then returned to the main street. Once inside his car, he composed himself a moment and thought about how to plan his strategy.

First, he called the police office in town and told Officer Stewart that the two men they were looking for might be seated at the local tavern. One of them fit the description that Stephen had given to the officer in his report. Also, one of the men was wearing a green jacket which also matched Stephen's description. It could be a coincidence, but it was worth investigating. After he got off the phone with the police, he decided the next thing to do was to return to the mission and talk with Rich and James. He pulled out on to the road feeling fortunate that he did not have to pass by the tavern on the way back.

Walking into the foyer of the mission, Andrew saw Joyce walking back to a hall closet carrying an armload of clean towels. "Where's Rich or James? I need to speak with one of them."

"Rich is out right now, but he should be back shortly. If you would like to talk with James, he's in his office."

"Thanks. That will do just as well." He headed down the hall.

James was on the phone. "No, we haven't seen anyone like that around here." There was a long pause. "Yes, he did have a tent, but I would have to ask him as to what kind." Another pause. "No, he's at the golf course today, but I will let him know when he comes in that you called. Bye." James turned around. "Andrew, come in. Sit down. What can I do for you?"

Andrew took a seat. "James, I just phoned the police. There are two men in a tavern in the village who match up to Stephen's description. To be on the safe side, we need to make sure that everyone knows about this and that the Hunters know the whereabouts of their kids. These men beat Stephen savagely and might have been the ones that robbed a store and there's something else. Someone is camping about a mile from here in a red domed tent. That's the same kind of tent Stephen was using. In fact, it might be the same one that was stolen. I asked the police to check into it."

James nodded. "I will call a meeting right now. I'll have Joyce call Rich to update him."

James headed to the other rooms to get the staff assembled. Andrew went into the lounge area by the fireplace to wait for the meeting to start. After everyone was gathered together, James repeated the information that Andrew had provided, then he continued. "These men are dangerous. We can't afford to underestimate where they might go or what they might do. We need to continue to keep doors and windows locked but also watch for signs of anyone on the grounds that might fit their description. Thanks in advance for your help in this. Let's pray. Lord, we thank you for your love and mercies. We know that ultimately you will vanquish all evil from the face of the earth. For now, Lord, we ask you to protect us, especially from these men. Keep us safe. May our shepherd defend us. In Jesus's name, amen."

The volunteers returned to their various places of work, expressing their individual concerns. Joyce approached James. "I called Rich and told him what happened. He's with Mark right now at soccer practice. Eric is playing in his room. My husband and I will have a serious talk with the boys this evening so they understand." She turned and gave Andrew a grateful look. "Thank you so much for keeping your eyes open and reporting this."

Andrew smiled, nodded, and walked back to his room to think.

Dinner was quieter than usual that evening, but Stephen did share the news with Andrew that he and Kenzy had a wonderful day of golf and conversation. Both of them had scores in the low 90s, not bad for two amateurs. More importantly, Kenzy had opened up to him about her deep aspirations. Likewise, Stephen shared his desired ambitions. As a result, the two of them had developed a stronger rapport. It sounded like there was room in her life for a new, meaningful relationship, the best news Stephen could hear. James informed Stephen of the phone call from the police. Upon getting the news, Stephen excused himself from dinner, contacted the police, and provided them with additional details about the robbery. Afterwards, he returned to the dining hall.

The boys acted a bit fidgety in their seats, since hearing the news about the two men. Their parents understood their anxieties. After all, they had witnessed firsthand the results of the brutalities inflicted on Stephen.

Rich and Joyce, although concerned, tried to remain as optimistic as possible. They were hoping this would help set a positive tone for the boys. Rich and James talked about next Sunday's sermon.

Andrew mainly focused on his meal, quietly running scenarios through his head about how he would respond if trouble arose. If anything should happen here at the mission, he was not going to end up like Stephen on his fateful afternoon. Andrew would never willingly assume the role of the innocent victim.

Chapter 9

On Thursday, by mid-morning, the staff and guests seemed a bit more at ease. The police had called the mission house to speak with Andrew and the pastors and informed them that no one was at the campsite he had spotted, but officers would remain vigilant. Unfortunately, the two men in the restaurant did not stay and order anything. According to the bartender, they sat down, talked a few minutes, and then for some unknown reason got up and left so the police had nothing to go on from Andrew's report, since they could not verify the identity of the two men.

After lunch, Eric and Mark went outside to play with some gliders. They were made out of lightweight balsam and floated easily along on a cushion of air. They invited Andrew to join them and made a contest out of who could fly the plane the greatest distance. Later, the game changed. Andrew would sail the plane through the air, and the boys would run to see who could catch it first. After about an hour of this activity, they decided to go inside and play with something else.

At that point in the afternoon, Andrew decided to relax on the patio alone, soaking up some afternoon sun. In Scotland, sunny days were a matter of hit and miss. They came; they went. Overcast days were commonplace, so when the sun actually came out for an entire day, locals rejoiced and reveled in it. Andrew was no different. He poured himself a cold lemonade and sat watching the horizon, bathing his mind in quietude, appreciating the peaceful setting. He closed his eyes and laughed to himself, thinking about the antics of the two boys. He began to doze off as he thought about the previous day's fishing trip and beauty of the woods and stream.

About fifty yards away, behind some brush, two men crouched down, looking at Andrew and watching to see if anyone else was around. There was no sign of anyone else outside.

"Are you sure that's him?" the first man asked.

"I'm positive, William. I don't know what makes you think I could forget that face. Any sign of those kids?" said Sam.

His accomplice shook his head. "No, not now."

Sam pondered a moment. "They might be his sons. I think they are back in the house now. Let's move in a bit closer."

William looked at Sam, feeling confused. "I don't understand. Why make this more complicated? Why not just shoot him now from here? Get it over with. Fast and simple. No one would ever know who did it."

Sam shook his head, revenge seething, burning inside his mind, rising like hot lava before the volatile explosion. "No, I want to see him suffer. I want to see the look in his eyes when he realizes his fate is sealed, trapped with no way out. Revenge is going to taste sweet."

In Sam's degenerate, uneducated mind, the only form of true progress equated to turning treachery into an elevated art form. These two coconspirators thrived on a steady diet of lies, deceit, theft, assaults, and homicides as if they were gourmet delicacies, none of which seemed to satiate their hunger for corruption. The two men maneuvered their way forward, keeping themselves hidden, staying low to the ground until they reached the patio.

Upon hearing footsteps on the stones, Andrew sat up.

Instantly, the two men rushed at him, knocking him backwards. The metal chair hit the stones with a loud clang. Andrew rolled to one side and jumped to his feet and, with his fist clenched, struck Sam in the jaw, sending him reeling.

The other man grabbed Andrew from behind pinning his arms. Stepping to one side, Andrew freed one arm, seized the man by the wrist and flipped him over, throwing him down on the patio. The man got up, staggered, and fell backwards, hitting the dining room window with his head and hand. He braced himself against the pane and then lunged at Andrew.

Upon hearing the commotion, Stephen and Rich ran outside, staring in disbelief at the brawl taking place. When Andrew saw them, between punches, he yelled, "Get out of here!"

Immediately, Rich ran inside, seizing Eric by his shirt collar in the process, who had come to the doorway and out of curiosity had stepped outside to see what the ruckus was all about. Rich saw his wife standing in the hallway looking perplexed, hoping for an explanation.

"Joyce, take the boys to the storage room and lock the door." Without wasting time to ask why, Joyce grabbed both boys by the hands and ran down the hall to the storage area.

Looking at the volunteers who stood standing there aghast, he yelled, "Get to the kitchen, lock the door, and lie down on the floor." Running to his office, Rich phoned the police.

At this point, William was dazed from repeated blows, but Sam had recovered. Getting to his feet, he charged into Andrew, slamming him into the kitchen window. Glass shattered in several directions. Although dizzy from the impact, Andrew managed to recover. Seizing one of the metal patio chairs, Andrew struck the man across his back with all his might. Sam went flying, landed in the grass, and rolled over, groaning.

Hearing the fracas outside, James appeared in the doorway and ran toward one of the assailants. As Sam's partner, William, attempted to take another swing at Andrew, James stepped in between them and struck the man across the face. William staggered and hit his head on the side of the brick façade. Glaring at James, animosity reaching its zenith, the man leapt on James, knocking him into the grass, giving him several hard blows to the face.

Sam, who had not been anticipating so strong a resistance from Andrew, reached for his pistol. Seeing the gun emerge, Andrew picked up a rock from the garden and hurled it at Sam full force, knocking the gun out of his hand. He yelled and held his throbbing wrist which had been rendered useless.

In the midst of the chaos, Stephen stood there, motionless and stunned, recognizing the two men who had robbed him. Sam's partner got to his feet. Looking at Stephen, he pulled out his pistol, hatred broiling in his face, and aimed. Simultaneously, Andrew took a flying leap, hurling himself at Stephen, knocking him backwards on the stone patio, the gun shot blast ringing in his ears. Andrew let out a scream as he fell, hitting his head on the patio, and landing alongside Stephen.

Hearing the police approach and commotion on two sides of the building, Sam yelled at his partner to run whereupon his accomplice grabbed him by the shirt, pulled him to his feet, picked up Sam's gun, and fled, infuriated that they had not taken out the intended target. That would have to wait for another day. With their getaway car parked just down the hill, the two assailants managed to jump in their vehicle and drive away.

Sam's partner was disgusted. "You should have just shot him when you had the chance. Now they've both seen us."

Sam glared at his partner. "William, this isn't over yet. Besides, all I really want is Schafer. We've seen that kid out back with him for several days. If we can get that kid, he'll come looking for him or at least someone will. That's our bargaining chip: the kid. We watch; we wait. We get our man and the kid lives. We don't, we get rid of the kid. He'll suffer either way."

"What do you mean? How do we get rid of the kid?"

Sam scowled at him. "What difference does it make? We can shoot him. We can throw him in the river and drown him for all I care." A sinister sneer gradually spread across Sam's face as he analyzed that idea for a moment. "That's it. We get the kid, make sure we're followed down to the river, and then we negotiate. You know what I mean? As soon as we get Schafer out in the open, we take him out."

"We could get into a shooting spree with the police."

"Idiot, the odds of our getting caught are good now anyway, and we already have a death sentence on our heads. What difference does it make? At least this way, maybe we take Schafer down with us. Besides, with one of us holding a kid hostage, they'll watch what they do. They won't risk killing the kid."

As they drove on, the two of them planned the details of their strategy.

Meanwhile, while several officers in a police car attempted to chase down the suspects, two officers assisted James to his feet. He suffered from some cuts, and his jaw was bruised. Another officer came to Andrew's aid. Stephen slowly rose to his feet, staring in bewilderment, amazed at his friend's fortitude. The bullet had ripped through Andrew's shirt and lodged in his left arm. Blood was running down the sleeve and on to the back of his hand.

The officer looked up at Rich who was standing in the doorway, looking sorrowfully at Andrew. "Call a doctor. Somebody, get something to stop the bleeding." Rich returned to his office to make the call to Dr. Campbell. James ran inside and came back with some towels. He knelt down and pressed them against the wound. Andrew gasped and winced.

Stephen stared at Andrew. "He'll recover, won't he?"

"He should, if he has no other injuries," the officer said. As he began checking Andrew over for other signs of blood or trauma, Stephen explained to the officer that the two assailants were the same men that had attacked and robbed him the previous week. Upon hearing that, the officer told Stephen to phone the police station immediately and provide all the possible details. Stephen complied and headed for the phone.

Two hours later, everyone was assembled in the lounge, waiting to hear news about Andrew's condition. James paced a bit about the room, wondering what to do next depending on the outcome. The two boys sat between their parents, looking anxious. Stephen sat still, staring at the wall, feeling numb. Kenzy sat beside him, holding his hand and giving him reassuring glances.

Finally, Dr. Campbell came out and addressed the group. "Andrew is going to recover. He's sleeping right now. He was rather fortunate in one sense. For some reason, the bullet did not penetrate too deeply, so it was easy to remove. The other good news is the arm isn't broken. He has a minor bruise on one side of his head, but the swelling should go down in a day or two at most. He's sleeping right now. I gave him some medication for pain. He is going to need rest. Someone will have to change that bandage tomorrow."

"Thank you again, Doctor. Your services are truly invaluable. I don't know what we would have done this past week without you," said Rich, looking extremely relieved.

Turning to the group, Rich said, "Thank you for responding so quickly in the midst of that chaos. The situation could have been much worse. The police are doing all they can to track down those two men. James and I will work out a schedule for monitoring Andrew for the next couple of days. If anyone else would like to assist us, that would be appreciated."

Stephen, feeling guilty for his friend's current state, raised his hand to get Rich's attention. "I would be glad to do anything I can for him."

Rich smiled. "Of course, thank you." He understood how close the two had become and realized how stressful this had to be for Stephen. After all, Andrew was like family to all of them.

That evening, Stephen skipped dinner. Instead, he sat by Andrew's bedside, grateful for his friend's heroic act. He had to tell Andrew the moment he woke up how indebted he felt. Stephen curled up in a chair and eventually fell asleep. Morning could not arrive soon enough.

By sunup, Andrew began to stretch and turn slightly and found Stephen sitting across from him smiling. "I guess you and I had another great adventure, didn't we?" said Andrew somewhat jokingly. "Next time let's just stick to fishing. It's easier."

Stephen was almost too emotional to speak. He sat staring at his friend. "Andrew, how can I thank you?" asked Stephen slowly.

Andrew stretched again. "Don't worry about it, Stephen. Friends do crazy things for each other sometimes." With a more serious expression, Andrew asked, "Did they catch those two thugs?"

Stephen shook his head. "I'm afraid not. Somehow, so far, they have eluded the police. They're hiding out somewhere. It's just that no one has figured out where yet." He paused. "Andrew, those were the two men who robbed me."

Andrew sighed and looked up at the ceiling. "I was afraid of that, but it doesn't surprise me any."

Stephen thought for a moment. "Andrew, I don't understand. Why doesn't it surprise you? And another thing. I can easily fathom why those men might want me dead. After all, I am the victim of a felony. If I give a positive identification of them in court, my testimony could lock them up for years, but why would they want to kill you? That makes no sense to me."

At the thought of those two men, Andrew's expression combined disgust with anger. He became so preoccupied with his thoughts for a moment it was as if he had not heard Stephen's question. Finally, he said, "I've got to find those two. I have to fix this once and for all. I can't hide anymore. I can't sit here safe behind these walls. I can't pretend that everything is secure when those two maniacs are loose, free to kill again. I had my suspicions from the beginning, and you've confirmed them. I have to come up with a plan and act on it. There's got to be a way. This has to end."

Stephen sat in the chair, staring at Andrew, feeling completely baffled. "Andrew, what are you talking about?"

Andrew took a minute to compose himself. "We talked a few days ago about my coming here from Glasgow, how I had left my job and came here for a change. One of the main reasons I left was to put some distance between me and those two men. I wasn't planning on them escaping." He paused, gathering his thoughts. "Remember you said that when you were attacked that one man called the other one Sam? After seeing their faces up close, I can tell you for certain that one of them is named Sam. Sam Preston. And the other one, his accomplice, is William Miller. They're killers. First, they evaded capture in the states, then they eluded the police in Scotland. I helped pursue them and bring them to justice. They were captured and tried in Glasgow. Because their crimes in Scotland became a high-profile case involving a prestigious member of a community, the court proceedings were almost immediate due to pressure from the media and the general public. I know for certain all this happened because I testified against them in court. They were both convicted of several accounts of first-degree murder. Both men were given the death penalty, but somehow, they managed to escape while in transit to prison. Somehow, they ended up here. Somehow, they tracked me down."

Still perplexed, Stephen asked, "I still don't understand. What do those two men have to do with you? Why were you testifying against them? What happened?"

Andrew looked up at the ceiling again, took in a long breath, and let it out slowly. He turned his head and looked directly into Stephen's eyes.

"I saw those two men kill my father."

Chapter 10

Saturday morning, Andrew's arm was on the mend. His appetite had returned, and he was up interacting with others and eating once again in the dining hall. Stephen had not said a word to the others about what Andrew had revealed concerning the two assailants. Fortunately, Andrew felt compelled to give additional testimony to a police officer, specifically the names of the suspects and their murder conviction. All these details were added immediately to the local police files. Since the two men were wanted for other crimes, they had been placed on a high priority list by the investigative team.

At breakfast, Andrew was somewhat quieter than usual, but after what he had been through, everyone concluded it was quite understandable. Toward the end of breakfast, Eric sat down next to Andrew. Eric could tell that Andrew was not acting like his usual jovial self but wasn't quite sure how to cheer him up. Nevertheless, he decided he would try anyway.

Hugging Andrew around the neck, he asked, "Want to see my train set? It's got eight cars. It doesn't go fast, but you can pretend it does."

Andrew looked into Eric's sweet face. It was obvious that Eric's immediate goal in life was to make everyone around him as content as he was. "That's really kind of you, Eric. Thank you for thinking of me, but for right now, I just need to sit and think." Andrew gave Eric a hug.

Eric nodded. "I am going to go play with Mark. If you change your mind, let me know."

Stephen looked at Andrew for a few minutes, feeling a bit disconcerted. Andrew was still resting from his incident. Doctor's orders. Nevertheless, it was clear that even though he sat immobile, his mind was racing, trying to figure out a plan of action. He could not truly rest with those two men out there plotting against him. Somehow, he would rise up and meet the challenge.

"Andrew, how about sitting in the lounge and playing a game of cards?"

Andrew somewhat reluctantly said, "Sure. Why not?"

The two sat down in the lounge, dealing out the cards on the large coffee table. "How about five-card draw for starters?"

"That's fine," said Andrew. The game lingered on for about twenty minutes. From then on, every twenty minutes, they chose a different card game. The mission house was quiet. Everyone seemed preoccupied with some sort of activity.

Unseen by the household, William and Sam had made their way toward the rear of the house, slithering along on their stomachs like serpents waiting for an opportune moment to strike. About ten minutes later, they got their chance. Eric came out alone looking in the grass, trying to find his toy car. Sam grabbed Eric from behind and swung him up into his arms. Screaming, Eric tried to fight back. "Got you," said Sam. "It's the river for you kid." At the same time, William threw a rock through the kitchen window. The two men ran down the slope back to their car with Eric. The abduction had taken only seconds.

Inside, at the same moment the rock came sailing past her, Joyce let out a terrifying scream from the kitchen and dropped a glass. Stephen, Andrew, and Rich ran to Joyce to find her standing in front of the kitchen window, pointing outside. "Eric! They took Eric! Oh God!"

All three men headed outside just in time to see a black car drive off at the bottom of the hill. Upon reentering the house, Rich saw the rock on the kitchen floor and realized something was wrapped around it. Rich read the note aloud. "No police. Send Schafer to the bridge." He looked at Andrew painfully, then ran to the phone to report the kidnapping.

As they drove off, Sam said, "Check to see who follows us."

William looked doubtful. "You think he'll come?"

Sam let out a sinister laugh. "He'll come. I know how he thinks. He'll come."

Joyce had collapsed into a chair, sobbing. "I was watching him. He said he wasn't going to play outside. He said he was just going to pick up his toy car that he had left in the yard and that he would be right back. This is my fault. I should have gotten the car for him. I should have been more careful. I should have watched him more closely. This is all my fault." She put her hands over her face crying and shaking.

While Stephen attempted to console her, Andrew got up and headed for the door, grabbing his jacket and car keys. "I've had enough of this insanity. I'm going after them."

Joyce looked up alarmed. "Andrew, they'll kill you."

"I was deputized the day I offered to track those psychopaths down. It's about time I did. It's me they want, not Eric. Enough talk. I'm out of here."

Andrew ran out front to the car and took off in the direction he had seen the black sedan traveling. He floored it, tires screeching as he roared down the driveway. He would go to the river, but on his own terms, not theirs.

In the distance, Andrew made out their car and slowed down to maintain a safe distance. The two men were heading northwest in the direction of the river. At one bend in the road, taking some sharp turns recklessly, the black sedan swerved and just missed colliding with an oncoming car. After about five minutes, the car stopped in the middle of the bridge.

Seeing where they had parked the vehicle, Andrew killed the engine and coasted over to the shoulder, making sure the car remained under the coverage of trees and bushes. His dark green car was well camouflaged amid the dense summer foliage. Taking a pistol out of the glove compartment, he checked to make sure it was fully loaded, took off his jacket, and then quietly got out of the car, heading for the bridge. He moved slowly down the side of the hill, using trees for cover.

The two men stood by the front end of the car as their cover, watching for Andrew's vehicle to approach. After standing there for several minutes, eyes locked on to the road, William became agitated and confused. "Where is he? This doesn't make sense. Could he have come from another direction?" William began scanning the area. There was no car visible on the road. No sound of an engine.

"He's coming. I know he will. Just be ready." They stood poised by the car, pistols in hand. Several more minutes passed. There was no sign of him.

By this time, Andrew had maneuvered down the embankment and positioned himself underneath the bridge at one corner, listening to every word they said. He set his pistol down on a rock beside him and removed his shoes. He wasn't quite sure what they had done with Eric, so he didn't want to take a chance with a shootout, at least not yet. If Eric was hidden in front of the car with them, they might use him as a human shield. If they had him in the trunk or the backseat, a stray bullet could pierce the car and kill him. Andrew would not take that chance. So far, his plan had worked. Since the two men had kept their eyes on the road but could not spot the car, they had not noticed his clandestine approach.

"I thought he was right behind us," said William. The two stood there straining their eyes, trying to make out any movement or sign of the car. From their perspective, it was as if he had vanished, dissipated like a cloud into the atmosphere. The two men stood there baffled.

By now, Andrew had begun wading slowly into the river, swimming slowly and quietly underneath the bridge positioning himself directly under the car, trusting his instincts would pay off. Those two would not have brought Eric here unless they fully intended to drown him. They had killed four people already; they would not hesitate to kill one more. He continued swimming slowly. The natural rushing sound of the river's current as it flowed hitting the rocks blended in with any sound he made like a melodic mask. He had trailed these men before and had second-guessed them. He prayed he could do it success-fully again.

William became exasperated. "Look, if he's not coming, let's get out of here. You know they phoned the police. Let's just throw this damn kid in the river and get out of here." At this point, Andrew was close enough to hear Eric screaming and kicking the sides of the trunk.

Sam stood staring off in the distance. "He should be here. This is puzzling. Maybe he lost his nerve." Totally exasperated, Sam got in the driver's side of the car and started the engine. "William, get rid of that kid."

William walked around to the trunk and opened it. Eric lay their wide-eyed in terror. William grabbed him and hauled him out of the trunk. Eric screamed and kicked as hard as he could, flailing his legs, hitting the man in his chest and arms. His efforts proved futile. William glared at Eric. "Get lost, you brat," yelled William, as he dropped him over the edge, and then jumped into the car as Sam revved up the engine and sped off.

In that moment, Eric screamed, anticipating the pain of falling on to rocks in the cold water. Suddenly, Eric thought he must be dreaming. He saw Andrew lunging backwards in the water right underneath him. Instead of plunging into the water, he had landed safely in Andrew's open arms. "Hang on, pal." Andrew tucked one arm under Eric's shoulders and swam to shore.

Eric and Andrew climbed up on the embankment and sat there a moment looking at each other. Eric felt dazed and yet reassured. He ran into Andrew's arms, shouting, "Andrew, you caught me." Andrew breathed a sigh of relief, hugging Eric tightly. "Stay here a minute, pal. I need to go get something." He walked over to the rock and retrieved his pistol and shoes. He looked back at Eric and smiled, comforted by the fact that his little friend was alive and that his instincts had been right all along.

Hearing the approach of several cars, Andrew stood up. Two unmarked police cars had stopped by the bridge. Andrew waved at them. "The kid's fine." One of the officers got out of the car and walked toward Eric, delighted to find him unharmed. "Let's get you back to the house. No point in worrying your parents any more than we have to."

Eric turned and hugged Andrew again. Andrew kissed his cheek. "Take off, pal. See you later."

Eric joined the officer, got into the car, and began hitting the back of the driver's seat yelling, "Home, home, home."

Andrew looked at the other officer. "I'm going after those two. If you want to come, I could use the help." Officer Stewart nodded. He had checked his records and knew for certain that Andrew had indeed been deputized for this very mission. He felt privileged to work with him.

The two men got in the officer's unmarked car which at first glance did not look like it had a chance in a high-speed chase.

Andrew got in the passenger's side. "They headed over the bridge. Let's go."

Starting the engine, Officer Stewart looked at Andrew reassuringly. "It might look like a mere compact, but believe me, it doesn't drive like one."

As they drove, the officer quickly pointed out that this vehicle had been equipped with a specially built engine which included added intake and exhaust valves along with a modified gearshift to help maximize speed. In addition, the windshield featured bulletproof glass, and the doors had reinforced steel plates with ballistic nylon. Andrew looked relieved.

At a distance, they could see that the black sedan was traveling fast down a country road headed for the side of the mountain and began to head up a steeper incline. The police car closed in to get within firing range.

"A little closer," Andrew yelled at the officer, rolling down the window, and drawing his pistol.

The cars continued up the hill, facing several curves. The assailants fired two shots at the police car, one penetrating the outermost layer of the bulletproof glass and lodging in the windshield and the other nicking the side of the door.

Leaning out the window, hanging on to the door frame, Andrew fired, hitting William in the neck. He screamed and slumped forward in the passenger's seat. The next shot, aimed at Sam, missed. Andrew made the split-second decision to aim for the tires instead. The third shot blew out the right rear tire.

"Hit the brakes," Andrew yelled as he climbed back into the car. The officer slammed on the brakes, putting distance between them and Sam's car. The black sedan, traveling at such a high speed, lost control, careened off the road into the shoulder, crashed through the guardrail, and down the hill, striking a tree head on, exploding like a bomb blast, flames flying, smoke mushrooming up into the air. The sedan was instantly transformed into an incinerated coffin.

Andrew and Officer Stewart sat there for a moment in their vehicle, staring at the wreckage. Quietly, Andrew said, "It's done. It's finally over. That was for you, Dad."

Chapter 11

Back at the mission, Rich and Joyce sat together in the church, pleading with God for their son's safe return. Holding on to each other sobbing, they managed to offer up short prayers of hope. James sat down behind Rich and Joyce, putting his arms around both of them. "I know this looks bleak right now, but somehow I feel the Lord will keep Eric safe." Joyce cried bitter tears and buried her head in her husband's shoulder. She was inconsolable. James looked painfully at his friend.

"Rich, remember the night Mark was so ill he almost died? That looked hopeless too, but God delivered him from sickness. We sat up all night, and by morning, he was well. I believe God will use Andrew to deliver Eric from harm. I don't know how, but I have a peace about it that I can't explain."

With tearstained eyes, Rich gave his friend an appreciative look. "James, I am so grateful for your friendship and support, but right now, I would give everything I own to have that peace. I don't know why God would explain that so clearly to you and not to me."

"I don't know either, except to say that he knows what each of us truly needs, and whatever he does, it is for the purpose of drawing us closer to himself."

At that moment, the church door opened and a police officer walked in with Eric. Upon seeing her son, Joyce leaped from the pew with a shriek of joy, ran to Eric, and swooped him up in her arms, sobbing with relief. Rich embraced them both and kissed Eric on the head, quietly thanking God that their family had reunited. Facing the officer, he said, "How can we ever repay you?" James thanked the officer and gave Eric a hug. "So good to have you back."

The officer shook his head. "I really had nothing to do with it."

Eric looked into his dad's wondering eyes. "Andrew saved me. He caught me, Dad."

Rich stared at Eric, not sure how to interpret his son's words, but at the same time, he decided it didn't matter. Eric was home.

Noticing Eric's wet clothes, he said, "Sweetheart, let's get you into something dry and warm."

Joyce set Eric down whereupon he ran to his bedroom. Joyce followed after him.

Mark saw Eric in the hallway and hugged him. "You're back. Yes! Somehow, I knew you would be back. Wow, Eric. You got to play cops and robbers with real robbers! Wait till the kids hear about this at school!"

As the officer left, Rich sat down in the pew, trying to compose himself. "Dear God, thank you that Eric's back. I don't understand how, but it doesn't matter. Thank you." He rested his arm and head on the back of a pew.

A moment later, the front door opened, and Andrew walked in, heading for the closet for a couple of towels, still wet from his swim in the river. Upon hearing the door open, Eric ran to meet him and jumped into his arms. "You're back."

Andrew laughed. "Yes, pal. I'm back. Let me put you down for right now. I'm all wet."

Eric waved and ran back to his room to play with Mark. Andrew was back. That's all that mattered for now.

Joyce, sobbing, ran to Andrew and hugged him.

Andrew smiled. "Joyce, I'm soaking wet."

At that moment, Joyce could not have cared less if Andrew had been covered from head to toe in axle grease. She was determined to hug him for rescuing her son. Joyce, both crying and laughing at the same time, replied, "I don't care if you're wet! Eric told me what you did. Thank you!" She embraced him again with all her might.

Rich walked into the hallway from the side door of the church and stood staring a moment in awe. He then walked to Andrew and embraced him, tears streaming down his checks. "I don't know how you did it. I don't know what to say except thank you so much."

James stood there admiring Andrew. "Thank God you are back here unscathed."

A moment later, Stephen emerged from the lounge area and welcomed Andrew home. He had both feared the worst but had prayed for the best.

Amid all the accolades, Andrew excused himself to change into some dry clothes.

That evening, Andrew walked into the dining hall carrying Eric on his shoulders and sat him down at his usual place at the table. At dinner, all the details of Eric's rescue gradually surfaced. Everyone sat amazed as Andrew narrated the accounts of the afternoon and his plan to outwit the two kidnappers and the car chase that led to their demise. Eric added a few details from his experience, especially the moment when Andrew caught him. Rich sat there trying to remember who had come up with the famous line: Truth is stranger than fiction.

After dinner, Mark looked at Andrew and then turned to his father. "Dad, Eric and I want to do something special for Andrew."

Rich, glowing with fatherly pride, said, "That's a good idea, dear. What did you have in mind?"

Mark continued. "We wanted to give him something, but we don't really have anything a grown-up would want, so we want to sing a song for him that I learned in school. Eric knows it too. I taught it to him last week. Can we sing it for him? Is that OK?"

His father said, "Yes, but maybe you should ask Andrew too."

Smiling at Andrew, almost in unison, they asked, "Can we? Please?"

Andrew looked into their innocent faces and nodded. "Sure. Go ahead."

Eric and Mark got up from the table and stood in the lounge area, facing everyone. Mark took a step forward, bowed, and introduced their performance. "This is a Scottish folk song called 'The Northern Lights of Old Aberdeen.' We only learned the chorus so far in school. We'll have to learn the rest later. Sorry about that."

Eric shouted, excitedly, "Mark and I were both born there."

Mark gave Eric a stern look to be quiet, then he said quietly, "Ready?" Eric nodded. Smiling at Andrew, they both took a deep breath and began singing.

The northern lights of old Aberdeen
Mean home sweet home to me.
The northern lights of Aberdeen are what I long
     to see.
I've been a wanderer all of my life,
And many a sight I've seen,
God speed the day when I'm on my way
To my home in Aberdeen.

At the end of the short number, both boys bowed to Andrew and once again to the other members of their audience, who all applauded and cheered loudly, shouting, "That was wonderful. Bravo!"

Rich stood up. "That's such a wonderful chorus. Let's all sing it together."

Eric and Mark clapped, jumping up and down. Swaying back and forth, Eric and Mark led everyone in another chorus. When the song ended, they both ran over to Andrew, hugged him, and kissed him on the cheek. Mark resumed his place at the dinner table.

Eric, overflowing with gratitude, climbed on to Andrew's lap. With his little arms wrapped around Andrew's neck, he looked him in the eyes, and said softly, "That was for you. Did you like it?"

Andrew could barely breathe. He stared at Eric a moment and then hugged him tightly. Tears running down his face, he looked into Eric's eyes that were always so full of love and trust. Eventually, Andrew managed to whisper, "Yes."

Chapter 12

The next morning at breakfast, Stephen made a startling announcement. After speaking with Rich and James in several private sessions and some prayerful consideration, Stephen had decided to become a pastor there at the mission to assist Rich and James. Eventually, he hoped to move on to form his own mission in another part of Scotland or somewhere else in the world if he felt called to do so.

Andrew could see the satisfaction in Stephen's face. "I really wish you all the best with your work. I'm sure the Lord will use you to bless others."

Stephen looked appreciatively at Andrew. "Thanks for your support and for all you've done for me. I've known you such a short time, and yet it feels like ages, like we have always been family."

Andrew nodded. "I feel the same way. It's like having a brother my own age."

Stephen looked at Andrew appreciatively. Andrew had no idea how ironic those words were, since Stephen had felt the same connection with Andrew that he had once had with his own brother.

Kenzy walked in carrying a plate of eggs and bacon. She set it down in front of them. Stephen looked at her adoringly. "When you finish with your work, how about joining us?" She nodded and smiled at both of them.

"She's a beautiful woman, inside and out," said Stephen sighing. "She's one more reason I will love serving here."

Andrew placed the linen napkin on his lap and poured himself a glass of juice. "I have some good news too. Last night I put a call through to one of my father's associates in Glasgow. I told him the news about my dad's attackers. While we were discussing that, he asked me if I would consider going back to Glasgow for a corporate position with the possibility of significant advancement in management. He made me quite a nice offer. I thought about it and decided to accept. I'll be heading back that way as soon as I can pack and say goodbye to everyone."

Stephen looked sad. "I will really miss you. I know the boys will feel the same way for days to come. Rich and Joyce won't want to say goodbye either."

Andrew stared at his plate. "I know, but I feel like it's the best thing for me to do right now. Besides, I can come back and visit. Glasgow is only a few hours away."

That Sunday service was bittersweet for Andrew. As much as he enjoyed the worship and fellowship, he also knew it would be the last time he would see the Hunters, James, Stephen, and the two boys for quite some time.

After lunch, he packed up his suitcase. Rich insisted on carrying it to the car for him and said a few painful goodbyes.

Stephen stood in the doorway, sorrowful to see Andrew leave but glad he was headed off to do the work he loved.

Andrew looked at Stephen and said, "I've got something for you." He opened up the trunk and handed Stephen one of the fishing poles and two lures. "Make good use of them. Let me know what you catch. When I come back, we'll go fishing at Loch Lomond." He handed him a piece of paper. "That's my address and phone number. Share it with everyone. Keep in touch."

Andrew reached back inside the car and removed an envelope from the front seat. "One more thing, Stephen. I thought you would want to have this."

Stephen took the large, white envelope and opened it to discover a color photo of himself and Kenzy standing in front of the clubhouse, their memorable golf outing, their first date. Stephen gave him a grateful look.

"Andrew, thank you so much. I am going to treasure this. That was thoughtful of you to think of us, especially with all the chaos you encountered." Andrew smiled. "Think nothing of it."

Stephen waved goodbye. "Thanks for the fishing gear. I'm looking forward to that fishing trip."

Mark gave Andrew a hug. "Thanks for playing with us. I hope I see you again."

"You will," said Andrew.

Eric ran outside and hugged Andrew, on the verge of tears. "You have to come back. You have to come see me. You're one of my best playmates."

Andrew hugged him. "I will. I promise," giving him a kiss on the cheek.

"Really?" asked Eric.

Andrew knelt down in front of Eric, looking into those soulful eyes. "Remember my birthday wish? Well, this was it: to come back here, if I ever left."

Eric smiled and hugged him again tightly.

Andrew smiled and waved as Eric walked back to stand next to his father. "See you, pal."

Before Andrew could get back in the car, Rich came forward, camera in hand. "Let me get a shot of you with the kids." Eric and Mark did not have to be coaxed. Upon hearing their father's suggestion, they ran down the front steps toward Andrew. He picked both of them up, one in each arm and posed for the photo, then Emily stepped forward and offered to take a group photo of Andrew with the whole family along with James, Stephen, and Kenzy. In that moment, Andrew realized he had the makings of a future souvenir scrapbook.

Andrew got in the car, rolled down the window, and waved at the entire household who had gathered to see him off. Stephen stood there smiling with Kenzy by his side, holding hands. Andrew sensed that one day he would be receiving a wedding invitation in the mail. No surprise there.

As he looked at them, he thought of the many blessings he had received in just the past week. He had enjoyed confiding in Rich and talking with him about his father. Rich was the only one there who knew the true purpose of his visit. He remembered the kindnesses that Joyce had extended and the inspiration of James's sermons. He relived rescuing Eric under the bridge and the beautiful song the boys had sung, a gift from their tender hearts that he would cherish forever. He also reflected on his decision to put himself between Stephen and a bullet. In that moment, he realized that was essentially what Christ had done for him. He thought about the fishing trip with Stephen who had told him: In every walk with nature one receives far more than he seeks. Andrew understood it was also true that in every close walk with Christ, one receives far more than one seeks.

He looked up again at the sign over the mission's doorway: Seek Ye First the Kingdom of God. As he drove off, Andrew knew that the Lord would graciously allow him to continue to discover more expressions of love and service in the months ahead than he could possibly ever hope to seek in a lifetime.

About the Author

Cynthia J. Sebring worked for thirty-two years as an educator in literary and language arts in Virginia. Over the course of her career, she served on numerous committees and advisory boards, including the Superintendent Teacher Advisory Council. She is a two-time recipient of the Congressional Youth Leadership Council Award. Prior to her years as an educator, she worked in private industry on contracts and various in-house articles for the US Navy as a writer and editor, as well as a consultative subordinate to research analysts.

As a graduate student of English, Ms. Sebring completed an editorial internship at a branch of the National Institute of Health (NIH) in the field of neuropharmacology, focusing primarily on compiling and revising medical research projects. As part of her undergraduate program, the author spent a summer abroad studying German literature and language acquisition at the University of Trier. Ms. Sebring has traveled extensively throughout Europe, the United States, and Canada, and she frequently uses these experiences as sources of inspiration.

The author has earned several master's degrees from the following institutions:

MA Theology, Christendom College, Front Royal, VA
MA English, George Mason University, Fairfax, VA
MA Education, University of Phoenix, Phoenix, AZ